Reparations
CORE

PHILIP WYETH

Also by this author:
Reparations USA
Reparations Mind
Reparations Maze
Chasing the Best Days
Hot Ash and the Oasis Defect

Cover design by Philip Wyeth.

www.philipwyeth.com

CONTENTS

1. The Wrong Picture ... 1
2. Money on the Table ... 8
3. Heard Some Rumors ... 13
4. Honoring a Theme ... 17
5. Edge of Treason ... 23
6. A Better Man Than I ... 28
7. Too Much Truth ... 34
8. Dreadful Silence ... 39
9. Who Could Refuse? ... 45
10. Broader Implications ... 49
11. One of Us ... 54
12. All Them Funerals ... 60
13. Forever Home ... 64
14. Temptation ... 70
15. Heads Will Roll ... 80
16. Surrounded by Fools ... 88
17. Paralyzed ... 94
18. Historical Landmark ... 98
19. Private Audience ... 105
20. Riding the Wind ... 111
21. The Brightest Star ... 115
22. Secret Thrill ... 123
23. Predator and Prey ... 126
24. Falling Away ... 131
25. More Primitive ... 135
26. It Ain't Fair ... 139
27. A Shine on His Soul ... 143
28. Suddenly ... 148
29. Going Underground ... 153
30. The Loneliest Revelation ... 166
31. Unchained ... 179

1. THE WRONG PICTURE

A spotlight flashed on and illuminated a tiny portion of the sound stage. A handsome white man in a striking gray suit stood with his head bowed.

Over the loudspeakers a voice shouted, "Ah-one, two, three, fooooah!" and big band music filled the air with a rollicking, upbeat tune.

The man on stage threw out his arms and looked up —the face golden tan, smiling teeth blinding—then began to frantically dance in time with the music. He performed a series of sophisticated tap dance moves, although his shoes made no sound. He held a triumphant pose as the final note rang out.

There was manic applause as the main lights came on. The man ran toward the side of the stage and caught a pencil-thin microphone that was flying in the air toward him.

Trotting back to the middle, he said, "Boy, oh boy! We're baaaack!"

Another eruption from the crowd, which slowly morphed into a low rumbling chant of, "DDM! DDM!

DDM…"

"Oh yes, you know it, folks. Ryan Richards back again with you on a Saturday night. *DDM TV Live* is locked and loaded and here to spread the good news. Eileen Jeffries-Lao—*la presidenta* herself—has been re-elected for four more years. Ooh, ooh, ooh… can you just taste the sweetness?!"

A handful of affirmative catcalls came flying back from around the packed studio audience.

"And Lord knows, if she's back and *DDM* is back, then we darn well better up our game. That's why we've got something new for you on tonight's show. A little sizzle to up the ante during these complex, *interesting* times. Are you ready… to get… *willllld?!*"

The percussive thump and low chants of a tribal ceremony echoed throughout the studio. Ryan Richards took a wide stance, placing a hand on each thigh as he bent his knees, then stomped and grunted his way around the stage.

The mighty blast of a baritone horn and two cymbal crashes sent him scurrying in mock-terror to a corner of the stage. He cowered even lower when a bird of prey's fierce cry filled the air.

Richards fought through his fear and glanced through trembling fingers at the huge screen that was above the stage. It displayed the *DDM TV Live* logo in a bamboo font. The flowing cursive words below it read, "Walk a Mile on the Wild Side."

Ryan Richards pretended to hack through a jungle as he made his way back to the middle of the stage. At last he fully recovered his confidence and addressed the rapt crowd.

"Dearest fans, here at home and around the world. For two full seasons we've dished out the healing balm to put old grudges into the dustbin of history. We've built bridges between the races after centuries of feud and abuse.

"However," the host continued, as he began to saunter across the stage, "so far all the work we've done has been along the clear-cut lines of color and ethnicity. *But!* Tonight that's all about to change. Strap yourselves in, ladies and gentlemen, because I'm about to blow your minds and expand this rail service right into your souls. Say it with me now. Wild, wild, wild, wild…"

The crowd began stomping their feet and chanting in unison. "*Wild, wild, wild, wild…*"

Images of chains and beaches and spears and wooden ships flashed across the large studio screens. The sounds of whips cracking and terrified screams grew louder and louder, until Richards flung out his arms and shouted, "Enough!"

In the anxious silence that followed, he lowered his voice and said solemnly, "If you can take it, I'd like you to meet Mr. Emile Smalls. Fourteenth generation Afrigro-American, whose family has seen the highest of the highs and the lowest of the lows. But through it all, they've shown grace and the survivor's spirit. Emile, come on out here!"

A slim black man wearing khakis and a polo shirt with bright stripes waved to the crowd as he walked briskly across the stage. He gave a smile and shook the host's hand.

"How are you, fine sir?" Ryan asked.

"I'm great. A big fan of the show."

"Is that right? Splendid! Then you're familiar with how all of this works?"

Emile gave a thumbs-up. "Of course. This should be fun!"

Ryan Richards turned to one of the cameras and

smirked. "Oh, and it *will* be. Now, Emile… meet your Direct Descendant Match!"

The face and ancestry profile of a middle-aged black woman appeared on screen. The crowd gasped and murmured. Someone called out, "You made a mistake! That's the wrong picture!"

Ryan wagged a finger in the direction of the heckler. "Now, now. Hold your plow horses…"

"But I don't understand," Emile said. "This isn't how DDM works. Shouldn't that be a Cauc up there?"

"Let me let you all in on a little secret," Richards said. "In some ways, those naughty boys working for the Sentinels of Jubilee were on to something. Maybe MARVIN *would* keep digging and crunching the data. Can you guess what he found?"

Emile shook his head.

"Come on," Ryan prodded, "take a stab."

"Is that lady part-white?"

"No, sir! Not only is she one-hundred-percent of African descent—nice rhyme, eh?—but we have concluded beyond a reasonable doubt, that in 1746 her ancestors on the Ivory Coast sold *your* entire family into bondage!"

"No way…"

The audience nearly fell out of their seats in shocked confusion.

"That's right," Richards continued, "captured them all and dragged 'em on down to the shore. Handed them over to the European merchants to be shipped off to the colonies abroad."

Emile was pacing in circles. He ran his hands over his face several times. Finally he mumbled, "I don't even know what to say."

"Well, you'd better think of something, because here she is… Connie Doumbia!"

A woman of forty, dressed in green cashmere sweater and dark blue jeans, reluctantly entered from the other side of the stage. Her eyes were cast down. The crowd, which normally went crazy when *DDM* contestants were introduced, now offered subdued applause.

Ryan Richards motioned for Connie to approach. "Come on over, it's okay. We're all friends here. Emile, can you say hello and shake hands, please?"

After the two guests had exchanged a silent greeting, Ryan said, "My, my. What ever should we do? Connie, are you feeling okay?"

The woman shrugged her shoulders. "Actually," she said through a mild African accent, "I'm in shock. I worked so hard to come to this country—legally!—fifteen years ago. How can this be happening to me?"

"Oh, I know," Ryan said, offering her a gentle pat on the shoulder. "But rules are rules—and ratings are ratings! Now Connie, your people did a *very* bad thing to Emile's family way back when. Would it be too much, after all these years, to finally say you're sorry?"

"*Me*, apologize? I don't know this man. He seems happy, in good health. How can anything I say make his life better?"

"Maybe we should ask him then. Emile, what do you think?"

Emile brought a hand to his chin and looked down in thought. Then he said, "You know what, Ryan? I just got a little bit scared."

"Why's that?" the host asked. "Are you frightened of *her?* Don't worry, I'll protect you!" Richards made a show of standing between Emile and Connie as if breaking up a fight.

"No, no," Emile said testily. "This isn't any fun! I was expecting... something else!"

"Hey," Ryan said, "times change." He gave a pained, wry smile.

"So *DDM TV* could be like this from now on? Brothers and sisters going against each other?"

"As well as Latizos, Tribal Americans, perhaps even people from Asia. Because apparently, our charter has… expanded."

The audience, which had been sitting in confused silence, now began to hurl boos and curses. Ryan Richards put up his hand and tried to placate them.

"Come on, folks," he said. "This show has always been about courage. Having the strength to look at our flawed history without fear, and then do what it takes to make amends. We don't get to set the boundaries of where this journey begins and ends."

Connie said, "What are we supposed to do now? I have two children in high school. I need to help them get ready for their college applications. I cannot leave with this man to do whatever it is you would have me do."

Richards put a hand to his ear. He nodded several times. "*I think—*"

"Just stop," Emile said. "I have an idea."

"Huh, really?" Richards was getting flustered. "And what would that be?"

"Ryan, you know I love the show. You're the best, man! But this is all getting too weird. Look, I don't want to punish this lady…"

"What *do* you want then? I mean, we have to do *something*."

"Connie," Emile said, "I would like to invite your family to have a cookout with mine. It's my mother's birthday next month. Let's all get together and have a nice time."

"Hmm," the show host said. "Sounds tasty." He

slowly shifted his gaze toward Connie. "Ms. Doumbia, what do you say to that?"

"Well," Connie said, "that would be lovely. Then at least we can turn this foolish use of people's time into something positive."

Ryan's face flashed a beaming smile. He spread his arms wide and pulled Emile and Connie in close.

"How about that, world?" he said with renewed confidence. "*DDM TV*. *Defying* expectations. *Dramatic* turns of events. And… *Magnanimous* examples of the *humane* spirit. Why don't we all take a quick breather? Then it's back to more unforgettable DDM showdowns after these commercials."

The audience, heartened by this pleasant outcome and hopeful of more-predictable Direct Descendant Matches to come, cheered enthusiastically once again. The stage lights faded out.

2. MONEY ON THE TABLE

Dawna Jenkins stood in the back next to the closed-up bleacher seats. Her arms were folded and she unconsciously nodded her head from time to time. Slowly she turned and surveyed the scene of this indoor block party.

Kids were running around the Newark rec center gymnasium having fun. Others played games like beanbag toss or were doing arts and crafts. A few police and paramedics kept a watchful eye. And Clyde was up there in the middle of it all singing his heart out.

"It's sell your soul to sing the Super Bowl. Keep it real? No endorsement deal…"

The dozens of people milling around from vendor to vendor sometimes turned to the stage and raised the roof. Others stood right up against the small stage and grooved along with DJ Clydoscope.

Dawna turned away to go see about getting some hot cocoa from one of the food sellers. She saw a wispy little white man dart out from one of the interior doorways. He flashed her a smile from under his mustache.

"Oh hi, Ms. Jenkins," he said, taking her hand into both of his own. "It's so nice to meet you!"

Dawna looked down at the man suspiciously and freed her hand. "Are you lost? You sure you know where you are?"

The man brushed some imaginary dust away from his wool trench coat. He nodded in the direction of the stage. "Pretty good singer, eh?" he said.

"He's doing alright. Lot of echoes in here though."

"Still, it's good to get another show under his belt."

Dawna flashed her eyes back at the man. Suddenly the tension in her forehead eased.

"I know who you are," she said. "Shoulda recognized. Just didn't expect to see you *here*, I guess."

The man extended his right hand in a formal greeting. "Dawna, it really is a pleasure to finally meet you."

She gave a half smile, saying, "You too, Mr. Pryor."

"Please, it's Eddie." He motioned for her to walk with him. "Let's get some refreshments, have a little chat."

"You want to talk to *me?* What about Clyde?"

"Oh, most definitely you. You're the adult in the family, right?"

Dawna readjusted the purse strap on her shoulder. "Trying to be. But of course, *he* doin' what he want. But whatever... I'm just rolling with all the changes. Even my friends be treatin' me differently now, too."

"How so?" Eddie nibbled on a toothpick as they neared the food vendors.

"They all seem to need some sort of help now. Calling on the phone with sad stories. Comin' around the new house..."

"Ah," he said. "Can I buy you a coffee?"

"Cocoa. Thank you."

A few minutes later, after they'd gotten their drinks, Eddie said, "Ms. Jenkins, the reason I'm here is simple. I—we, my team—we think Clyde has tremendous potential."

"I always knew he was talented."

"Indeed. And he's got fire! Which, I think, expressed itself again when he went his own way on the new song."

Dawna stopped walking. Her eyes grew distant. "That one ain't doing too well."

"It happens. 'Soul's Gold' wasn't *bad*, but maybe the concept just went over people's heads. It was *kind of* fun, *kind of* smart, *kind of* emotional. He'll learn over time."

"I hope so," she said, moving forward again. "But he's still a kid. They do what they want to."

Pryor gave a gentle smile. "No one wants to listen to us older folks. What do we know, right?"

"Huh! Only how many ways to Sunday life can hit you."

"I'm glad you said it. That's why I came to you directly. Clyde... he's raw. But at some point he's got to *refine* that energy if he wants to stick around in the spotlight."

At that moment the music stopped. Dawna turned around and watched Clyde up on the stage wave to the small cheering crowd. She said, "Maybe he only wants this. Maybe he's okay singing to the local kids."

Pryor shook his head and looked down. "But you know better. *Your* hands are tired. I think you'd be doing your son a disservice by letting him walk down the path that ends with him waking up at age fifty, looking back at what could have been, if only."

Bringing the insulated cup to her chest, Dawna said, "I know we all got to make our own decisions, but when there's money on the table…"

"And family to think about."

"Mm-hmm."

"Will you talk to him?"

"Ooh, I don't know. He seems to think you won't let him be him."

"I'll put it to you this way. We work with artists of all stripes. Yes, it's *easier* for us if the talent wants to play ball. We plug them right in to our setup and then everyone's off running. But, in the case of someone like DJC," Pryor said with a wave, "we can paint the whole thing as 'the defiant genius at odds with his artistically illiterate management,' and such."

"Hmm," Dawna sniffed. "So you got all your bases covered then?"

"Ma'am, I make money for a lot of people. And look, I may not be an innocent little choir boy, but I do always approach those I want to work with straight. Clear and to the point. I want everyone to be *happy*. That way we all prosper, and no one's looking over their shoulder afraid the last person they burned is coming to take revenge."

Dawna sighed. "Thank you for saying that. But no matter what, I'll always be watching!"

"Please, Ms. Jenkins. Talk to your boy. You know that life doesn't stand still just because you want it to. After the success of 'Fly So High,' he can't just do it all in a vacuum according to his own whims."

"There's a lot of folks who want to work with him, though. Really, why should he go with you—a white man—when there's plenty of brothers who be knockin'?"

Eddie spread his arms in supplication. "Because if I

screwed him over, you would show me no mercy. There's no gray area when dealing with someone like me—it's true black and white, eh? I can't get away with anything. You wouldn't let me."

A smile fought its way through Dawna's clenched teeth. She nodded. "Okay. I'll sit him down. It's time to hear the facts of life that he didn't—couldn't—learn on the street."

"Wonderful, just wonderful."

"But if I get him to do this, and I *ever* catch a whiff of something…"

Eddie Pryor shook his head, looking up at Dawna with puppy dog eyes.

"Let's *all* make money," he said. "A lot of it."

3. HEARD SOME RUMORS

Chris Donohugh held the door open and Kate entered the clinic bundled from head to toe. It was freezing out, even by New York City standards for this time of year. Chris followed her in and pulled down the zipper on his own heavy leather jacket.

He stood to the side while Kate checked in at reception. A few months back in the swing of life and he'd forgotten this whole medical routine. The smiling staff, the cleanliness, all the *empty space* in these hospitals. As if the unspoken enemy, death and disease, would get lost and dissipate in the endless corridors.

Chris inspected Kate's face as she chatted away with the receptionist. She *looked* fine. But during those scary spring and summer months he had found himself going into some very dark places mentally. There was just no one to dump his husband's anxiety on—and he was mortified by even the thought of telling Kate, not when she was fighting her own battles. Today he suddenly felt that oppressive mood returning.

"It'll be just a few minutes," he heard the receptionist say.

Kate eased out of her long puffer coat as they walked over to the seating area. She dropped her things into a pile on a chair, picked up a random magazine, then sat down and threw one leg over the other.

"Here we go again," she said.

Chris poked around the selection of periodicals. "Do you want me to go in with you?"

"I don't think you need to. Just a scheduled checkup, right?"

"Let's hope so." Chris sat down next to her without taking a magazine. He put his hand on her thigh and gave it a rub. "How about we get something really greasy to eat later?"

Kate smiled. "Chinese. I want pork fried rice. And sweet-and-sour pork with extra sauce!"

"Okay, Porky," he grinned. "We'll eat our way through this cold front."

"Mm-hmm."

A few minutes later the door near reception opened and a nurse in pastel purple scrubs said, "Mrs. Donohugh? We're ready for you."

Kate picked up her purse and squeezed Chris's hand. "Be back soon."

She followed the nurse through a few hallway turns with the usual chitchat, then they entered an exam room.

"Please take a seat," the nurse said. "Doc'll be here very soon. But before she comes in, let me just do what I need to do."

Kate received the battery of pulse, eye, and other basic inspections. When the nurse said, "You haven't lost any weight, that's good," Kate looked at the reading on the scale a second time. Up *seven* pounds from her last doctor's visit. Still, Chinese food was definitely on today's menu.

"Hi, Kate!" It was Dr. Lowell. Six feet of spunky energy that had helped Kate get through the whole ordeal. "How is everything?"

Kate leaned in and gave her a hug. "It's so nice to see you. Things are… good. Really good."

"That's so great to hear. Let's run through this and get you on your way then."

"Are you going out of town for Tribesgiving?" Kate asked while removing her shirt and bra.

"Oh, yes. We'll be taking the kids to my in-laws' country house in Upstate." The doctor slipped on gloves and began to examine Kate's torso with deft hand movements. "And you?"

Kate, in between taking long even breaths, said, "Visiting Chris's parents in Maine. Which means we'll be headed down to DC to spend the Holy Holidays with my family."

"How wonderful."

"Although," Kate sighed, "fingers crossed, I might be doing some work down there as well."

"In Washington? How's that?" Lowell continued to inspect Kate while they spoke.

"I've heard some rumors, let's just leave it at that. But it would mean more responsibility than ever."

"Well, you've been an inspiration this whole time. If your body stays cancer-free, I can't imagine that you'll have any trouble keeping up on the job front."

Kate looked down into her lap. "Dr. Lowell?"

"Yes, Kate?"

"I… Lately I've been thinking about the possibility of having children."

The doctor smiled. "Hey, now!"

"But, I need to be sure that my body will… for both

me and the baby."

"Kate, the best news is that in your case we caught it all so early. Plus, thank God, you didn't need chemo. Your body's recovery time—and affected area—was considerably less than if we'd had to go all the way."

"I know," Kate said, gratefully running a hand through her long hair. "It's just that between work, being older, and all this... I need to be sure I'm doing the right thing."

"Darling," the doctor said while snapping off the gloves, "thirty-three is not *older*. Now, let's get you X-rayed and back out into the world. Hmm. I'd love to see you as a mom!"

"Thank you."

"And you'd better bring little Baby Donohugh in to meet me, too."

Kate smiled as she pushed her arms into the patient gown, then followed Dr. Lowell toward the X-ray room feeling light on her toes.

4. HONORING A THEME

President Eileen Jeffries-Lao sat in stunned silence. She reread the diplomatic cable that had been received through private channels earlier in the evening.

"Madam President and your esteemed staff... After profound reflection... extensive consultation... regret to inform... conclusion that in our nation's best interest... will not be participating in a Reparations program... administration's inability to oversee this, your signature program... detrimental effects... the soul of your people...

"...our hope that the United States can one day return to its role as leader and innovator... your cultural priorities... pray that you will course-correct... With sincere regret, but with hope for other cooperation in..."

Jeffries-Lao felt hollow and numb. Her stomach was tight and when she went to stand up, she found that her free hand held the armrest in a death grip.

After a moment of slow breathing to calm herself, Eileen walked over to the secure phone that was on a tiny table next to the door. When the crisp, subdued male voice on the other end of the line answered, she said, "The Philippines has declined our invitation to the dance."

"I see," the man said after a brief pause. "What do we intend to do in response?"

"I do believe that rampant green card fraud has been going on for years unchecked. Start there. Let's see the reaction when thousands of their citizens are deported —*and* the money being sent home dries up."

"Very good. For your information, 'unchecked' does not necessarily mean 'unobserved.' We know who's out there, ma'am. Just give me a number…"

Eileen took the curled black phone cord into her fingers. She looked at the small diamond-shaped mirror hanging on the wall nearby. "Start with three thousand."

"How do you want us to handle… the optics?" the man asked.

"Hmm. I'm locked in for this second term, but the fight just got tougher. If this letter of regret is any kind of barometer, then other countries on the fence are going to want to see strength. Resolve."

"Consider this, Madam President," the man said. "After word spreads about this order, there will be cameras rolling every time we arrest someone. How humane will the Reparations president look when she's seen rounding up families in the dead of night?"

Eileen uttered something that was more of a grumble than a sigh. After a moment she said, "I guess we just need to remind the world that our generosity doesn't necessarily go on forever. If the Filipinos want to play hardball against our offer to patch them into the HRA's ecosystem, that's fine. Let's flex our muscles until they realize that *we*, the United States, still set the terms of deals on the big stage."

"Understood," the man said. "I'll instruct the apprehension teams to do this as discreetly as possible. But in the case of..."

"Tell them to just do what they need to do, alright? I'll have my people ready to spin this thing any which way we need to. No one can compete with *our* PR machine."

"Consider it done. Give us one week."

"Thank you."

Eileen found herself staring into the little mirror long after she had hung up the phone. Her hand was up at her throat, fingertips tapping the beads of her necklace.

All that work. All of the *years!* She had given her life to honor... a theme. Serving those who could not speak for themselves. Performing the high-altitude work of coordinating with her privileged allies to wrangle the mishmash of society's outcasts into a patchwork coalition that could win elections.

Yes, Eileen acknowledged with a near-smile, the strict household of her Chinese parents had paid dividends. All of the rules, the discipline, the watchful eyes—a traumatizing experience when compared to the easygoing home lives of her white California classmates.

Decades later, it had proven to be the advantage that enabled her to rise politically while harnessing those same vain, pot-smoking, bleeding hearts to create real change. They could never have done it on their own. Eileen was the engine, the glue, the *prescient one* who saw how to bring the fringe idea of Reparations into reality.

Early on in local Orange County politics, she'd utilized her connections as a school board member to get a state-of-the-art homeless shelter funded. It was touted as offering a trifecta of benefits: humane treatment for the residents, student safety while walking to and from school, and keeping the sidewalks clear for business.

This successful outreach effort, which went far beyond the charter of her job description, had given Eileen her first taste of... not power, but the kind of results her influence could bring about.

No one had ever quite been able to pinpoint her secret. Eileen wouldn't have gotten anywhere had she run as a Rebellican, but as a Dramacrat she soared by following a simple strategy. Publicly she *leaned* leftward, but always made a point to acknowledge the merits of her opponents' concerns. This served to establish her reputation as a dignified, patriotic stateswoman early on in her political career.

Meanwhile, at private fundraisers and rallies, she also encouraged members of the Far Left to express their ideas openly. And later, when the party's diverse factions inevitably devolved into self-interested squabbles, the humble Eileen was there to offer a moderate-sounding platform that would, behind the scenes, still work to chip away at the more controversial issues over time.

A prime example of this took place in 2021 when she was the governor of California. She spearheaded a controversial outreach program which included two ancillary benefits for herself—bringing the Jeffries-Lao name to national prominence, as well as endearing herself to conservative women.

Her ingenious insight? As a counterbalance to the *pride* aspect of encouraging girls to pursue serious careers, she carefully crafted a message warning about the mental and physical health risks of *empowered* sex, which disproportionately affected women.

Eileen believed strongly that this nod to traditional life had convinced many Rebellican women around the country to vote for her in 2024—and therefore secured several swing states on her path to victory. Once again, the Chinese *cultural* influence had played a hand in winning a *political* victory, which not only made her ancestral homeland proud, but also eager to do business.

A few short years later and what had she become? The montage of photos chronicling how much a president aged while in office did not sufficiently capture the slow deformation of Eileen Jeffries-Lao's soul.

But she took some small solace in knowing that it wasn't about her anymore. She'd already done the impossible by getting this Reparations program codified. If the next four years had to be spent throwing haymakers in a slugfest to save the Historical Reparations Administration, so be it. She would rest later, much later.

Now the visage of one masked man entered her mind. She dreamed of the day when she might knock him to the dirt for his terrible treason against the crowning achievement of her life's work.

There were others as well. A growing list of defectors and those who had betrayed her. One former ally in Congress would soon be expelled and possibly put on trial—but that would all have to be handled delicately. If only he had been a Rebellican!

Hundreds of civil servants had also aided and abetted the Sentinels of Jubilee. Cowards! She had always loathed the types of people who thought they could bring about a revolution while simultaneously funding their 401Ks every two weeks.

And finally, she thought of the ingrates. All those

Beneficiaries who hadn't gotten their act together even after millions of dollars poured into their communities. Worse still, the likes of Clyde Jenkins and his promoter-enabler Nolan Simmons, whose homemade rap song had become a rallying cry whipping up discontent across the nation.

This was the first time in Eileen's life that she had ever felt such thirst for revenge. But of course in the past, there was always some next step forward to pursue. She had simply harnessed any negative energy inside her toward winning, leading...

But after all this, there would be no other hills to conquer. And Eileen Jeffries-Lao was too hungry and proud to just go quietly into the night. She would make a last stand at all costs.

5. EDGE OF TREASON

Victor Dominguez heard the phone ring but ignored it. He rolled onto his back and stared at the ceiling.

The attempted call had torn him out of a nightmare, but his waking thoughts in the week since the election had been no better. He pulled a pillow over his face, hoping to block everything out.

As he drifted back toward sleep, Victor heard the phone ring again. He turned his head and looked at the bedside clock—twenty past five. He wondered who the hell would have the nerve to call not once, but twice at such an early hour.

Victor reached over and took his phone off the table and disconnected the charger. Unknown number. He pressed to answer.

"Hello?" he said testily.

"Good morning, Victor."

"Who is this?"

"Let's just say, I could be a friend." The man's voice was crisp and clear, and had the staccato flair of an upper-class Spanish accent.

"Now listen," Victor said, "it's too early for games. What do you want with me?"

The man chuckled lightly. "Tell me, how have you been feeling lately? You know, post-election?"

"Look, I don't know who you are, so you'll get no free sound bites. But draw your own conclusions."

"I sympathize, truly. Or should I say, *we* sympathize." The man paused, exhaled. "Victor, how would you like the opportunity to… if not grab victory from the jaws of defeat, then perhaps take the reins of another powerful horse?"

Dominguez sat up in the bed. A glow of blue and yellow was creeping in through the hotel suite curtains. Quietly he said, "I came so close. Even when, for most of the campaign, no one gave me a shot. Or support…"

"We know it. My god! We were in *awe* watching how the sacrificial lamb almost became the shepherd. Which is exactly why I am calling you now."

"Please," Victor said, "what are you hinting at—or offering?"

The other man cleared his throat. "Did you happen to notice anything else of particular interest about the election night results?"

"Not really. I didn't have much time for anything, besides being there to support my disappointed campaign staff and voters. It's all been one sad blur."

"True, but you've still got two years left in the Senate before you're up for re-election. We can make that work. For everybody."

"How does that relate to the election we just had?"

"Victor, did you really not see the wave of Latizo candidates that just swept into office? Nationwide, at all levels, we are gaining real political power."

Victor Dominguez stood up and walked over to the room's small writing table. He sat down and flipped on the brass-topped lamp. "I'm sorry that I wasn't able to deliver the ultimate prize," he said faintly.

"Oh, but you have!" the caller replied. "This game has only just begun, Victor. And you proved by the way you handled yourself that you're just the kind of man we need to lead us."

"I really don't know what you mean. In fact, I still have the interests of my constituents to serve. I don't know if I can help you."

"Nonsense. Listen to yourself. Do you *really* think you'll be able to just go back to being who you were? Can your *mind* handle the downgrade to boring Arizona politics after that big talk about taking on the HRA?"

"I was defeated," Victor said, tapping a pen against a notepad emblazoned with the hotel's logo. "Besides, John Kerry did very well for himself later on after playing the good soldier."

The other man laughed heartily. "I'm not talking about waiting *four years* hoping to get a posh appointment. We want you *now*."

"Spit it out then. You've woken me up and still not said who you are or what it is you want with me."

"Senator Dominguez, we are interested in you because everything you said about the HRA was so true. More importantly, *we* don't need Reparations."

Victor's eyes widened and he felt his skin tingle. "Who's... we?"

"Latiz-Americans, that's who! We've been rising on our own merits this whole time. We don't need any of that redistributed money. Not if it ties us to the Afrigro-Americans as they drag themselves down. And definitely not if we want to be seen as equals on par with white people." The man chuckled. "Many of us do in fact have some Caucasian blood as well, you know..."

After a moment of silence, the caller said, "Victor? Are you still with me?"

"Yes," Dominguez whispered, running a hand back over his thinning black hair. "I hear you, but I still don't *see* where this is leading."

"Sir, we are strong! It is time for this Latizo coalition to flex its muscles out in the light of day."

"So, what? Do you want to have a parade, or for me to sponsor a bill setting aside a day in our honor?"

"Don't be ridiculous. I'm talking about us having the power to act *right now*, as if you were in fact president."

Victor let the pen fall from his fingers. That cruel illusion of hope, which he had foolishly allowed himself to indulge in the home stretch before Election Day, now slithered back into view. He said gravely, "This kind of talk is getting very close to the edge of treason. You'd better assure me that you're not thinking of trying something that could get a lot of people... punished."

"No, no," the man said with a heavy breath. "Eileen Jeffries-Lao will remain as president unless she chooses to leave office of her own free will. But... now that she has survived this scare from you, her administration will be doubling down on expanding the HRA into new territories. Their logic being, of course, that the more franchises they open, the less likely anyone will be able to shut down the original terrible idea."

"Do you want me to take to the Senate floor and filibuster against those plans?" Victor asked.

"I'm afraid that won't be a firm enough message to send. Not when you're just one lonely voice out of a hundred. No offense, my friend. Let me say it again— Latizos are rising. The last thing we want is for the

HRA to get its tentacles spread all across Central and South America. We must not let our people be corrupted by that mental poison!"

"Oh my God…"

"Glory, not grievance, Victor!" the man rasped. "*Reconquista*, not *Reparaciones!*"

The line clicked dead. Victor Dominguez sat shivering at the desk in his boxer shorts and t-shirt. He watched the light of the dawning day slowly flirt with the edges of the curtains. Soon he would call room service and order the strongest coffee on the menu.

6. A BETTER MAN THAN I

The Reverend Matthias G. Witherspoon saw them poking out above the dozens of RVs that were parked beside the road. As he slowly drove his green Cadillac forward, the objects closest began to come into focus.

Steel structures of the prefabricated, quick-build variety dotted the landscape. And a half mile beyond them stood his destination—the Mall of Absolution in Bloomington, Minnesota, where he had accommodations and appointments already booked.

But even after the long drive in tough autumn weather from his home in Akron, Ohio, Matthias was too intrigued by this spectacle to just go racing past. Because although he'd heard about how the Modestian headquarters had been bombarded with refugees, actually seeing this gathering of humanity in the flesh was overwhelming.

Matthias turned onto a makeshift dirt road that had been graded and which led to one of the steel structures. At the cul-de-sac, a man wearing a neon blue hardhat and jacket with silver reflectors hailed him to the side. Matthias pulled over then rolled his window down.

"Good afternoon," the worker said. "Can I see your papers and decal for this dormitory?"

Matthias blinked twice. "I, uh…"

"Sir, we've got a lot of people to process before this next cold front passes through. I'm happy to scan you in, but please try to keep things moving."

"Is this here all part of the church?" Matthias asked while waving his hand around. "Modestians put these buildings up?"

The other man smiled. "Yes, sir. A lot of these folks who showed up, well, they either came in the early fall or don't own RVs. There's no more space in the Mall, but we couldn't very well have them ride out the winter sleeping in their cars either. So, the Prescient One and the committee fast-tracked getting these dorms put up."

"But there are so many…" Matthias marveled.

"And we're still building more. About two a week. If they come, you will build it, eh?" The man grabbed the lip of his hardhat and chuckled. "Anyway, sir. No offense, but if you're just sightseeing I'm gonna have to ask you to move along so I can get to these folks behind you."

Matthias peered into his rear view mirror and saw that two old beater cars had pulled up behind him.

"Yes, of course," he said. "I'm actually headed to the Mall now. I have an appointment with Emissary Jacoby."

"Oh, my!" the worker exclaimed with genuine admiration. "In that case, please do get back on the main road and follow the signs in. You'll get a much better night's sleep in there compared to out here."

"Wonderful." Just as Matthias was about to close the window, he looked at the man and said, "You know, son. You really are doing God's work."

"Thank you, sir. And Mod bless *you!*"

Matthias pulled forward and swung around the end of the loop. He glanced to his right and looked inside the structure's large sliding door which was halfway open. The building, which was about the size of a high school gymnasium, was brightly lit and filled with people bustling around.

He saw cots and bunk beds, folding tables, and a cafeteria-style food setup before the motion of his car took the dormitory out of view.

The Reverend Matthias G. Witherspoon nodded to himself. Now he was certain about his decision to take a leave of absence from his own black church back home, so that he might meet these Modestians face to face. It was clear they did more than just *preach*. They solved problems—coordinating and cooperating—and did so with a positive attitude, rather than pretense.

About a quarter mile from the Mall itself, Matthias was taken aback when he came upon what looked like a border crossing. The road opened up into a fortified toll plaza, with armed guards keeping watchful eye as cars fanned out into the different lanes.

Matthias eased forward and pulled up next to one of the booths. A guard and a thick steel gate blocked his path.

The man sitting inside the booth looked up from a tablet and said, "Welcome, Reverend Witherspoon. How was your journey?"

"Fine, thank you," Matthias said. "How did you know it was me?"

"Plates and retinal scans. So fast, I know! We'll get you on your way in just a minute."

"Excuse me for asking but, what would have been the greeting if I was an unexpected guest?"

The officer chuckled. "I'm sure you'll understand if I don't reveal all of our security precautions."

"Of course."

"But let's just say, anyone who makes it inside the Mall is supposed to be there. We're not just a fun little group anymore. A lot of people see us as a threat now."

"So I've heard."

"But not to worry, Reverend," the man said pleasantly. "That just means you'll be safe and secure during your stay with us. And I do hope you find what you're looking for."

Matthias smiled. "I'm finally starting to understand why they say that God works in mysterious ways. Just a few months ago I was a much different man."

"I know the feeling. Well, we're glad that you've come. Now," the man said, pointing a finger beyond the gate, "once you pass through, pull on up to that little blue shack on your right. They'll instruct you where to go."

Matthias heard a heavy click and then saw the metal gate tilt back and down into a recession in the pavement. The guard standing in front waved him forward. Matthias drove past and approached a tiny outhouse a hundred yards up ahead.

A matronly woman in a glittering silver pantsuit stepped out and waved to him. She tried the passenger door handle but it was locked, so she politely knocked on the window and pointed down. Matthias pushed the button on his side panel to unlock the doors.

The woman opened the door and poked her head in. "Greetings, Mr. Witherspoon! May I?" She patted the empty seat.

"Of course," Matthias said.

"Thank you, thank you." She got in and closed the door. "Eldress Cameron. It's an honor to meet you."

Matthias shook her hand and smiled warmly. "Glad to make your acquaintance. I have to admit, I wasn't expecting such a fortified—or personal—reception."

"And this is just the beginning," Eldress Cameron said with a laugh. "Now, if you'll just continue down this road, I'll have you turn into the second parking structure. There's a VIP spot reserved just for you."

Matthias did as he was instructed and pulled into a multi-level garage that was adjacent to one section of the Mall itself. He drove up a ramp to the second floor, and then as he rounded a corner saw two dozen men and women in matching teal robes surrounding a parking space. He could see that they were singing.

Eldress Cameron motioned for him to enter the spot. He eased in very slowly so as not to accidentally bump against any of the choir members. When he opened his door, he heard the lovely hymnal "Come, Let Us Anew Our Journey Pursue" echoing through the garage. He joined Cameron in standing behind the car to admire the performance.

"O that each in the day of His coming may say, 'I have fought my way through...' "

Matthias clapped and gave a polite bow when the group had finished singing. "Thank you!" he said. "Wonderfully done."

Eldress Cameron began to lead him away, saying, "We of course have our own repertoire of original hymns, but thought it would make you feel at home— and see that our religions are not *too* distant from one another—if we sang something already known to you."

"A thoughtful touch, indeed. Oh," Matthias said, glancing back at his car. "What about my bags?"

"Reverend, please! You are our *guest*. All of your needs will be tended to." Cameron shook her head with a smile. "As if you would be expected to bellhop your own suitcases, Mod help us all..."

They stepped onto a covered walkway that connected the garage to the main structure. Two strongmen wearing teal-and-gray camo fatigues stood watch, each armed with a blue-turquoise ceremonial staff that was topped by a dense acrylic bulb framed in silver.

Matthias and Eldress Cameron passed through two sets of sliding doors, and then the interior expanse of the Mall opened up. Matthias marveled at the ornate banners and elegantly color-coordinated design. It felt as if the castle of a wealthy Medieval king had spread out over a million square feet.

As they proceeded, he saw that old storefronts had been converted into crafts rooms and gift shops. They passed a line of schoolchildren quietly streaming into the youth gymnasium. And over at a small table, several women in matching ash-gray robes were discussing what Matthias assumed to be the Modestian holy book. The gentle patter of an unseen fountain completed the picture.

He and Eldress Cameron rounded a corner and entered a main foyer. Matthias stood stock still. He brought a hand up to his chest. Cascading down from the skylight was a massive banner of the Prescient One giving a knowing smile. Matthias felt his heart shudder.

Eldress Cameron touched his arm softly and said, "Are you alright, Reverend Witherspoon?"

"Yes," he said. "Very. It just hit me that I'm really here, that's all."

"Come, then. The Prescient One himself is eager to meet you in person."

"Oh Lord, give me the strength…"

"Shush! He's still human, just like we all are."

"Maybe," Matthias said. "But he's a better man than I am."

"Let Mod be the judge of such things, Reverend."

7. TOO MUCH TRUTH

"Hold up, hold up. Rolling it back. Let's try it again."

Clyde Jenkins closed his eyes in frustration. This felt like the twentieth time that the producer had stopped the track and cut him off halfway through a line.

"Ready whenever," he said.

The music started again. A solid percussive hip-hop beat with hints of moody synths played in his headphones.

"She got that Ho'Spice. Naughty nurse, booty so tight. Ho'Spice, make me see the light. Ho'Spice, my sickbed's delight. Easy come, easy—"

"Cut, cut!" the producer growled. "Clyde, it's got to be more sexy, more smooth."

Clyde nodded at him through the studio glass. "Oh."

"Look, the dude in the song, he ain't *really* dying. He gettin' laid! But this girl be like a drug, you know what I'm saying?"

"No doubt."

"Say, DJC. You need a little, uh, spice of your own

to get into this jam?"

Clyde brought his hands together as if in prayer. He said, "Lemme just get this part. Then maybe, yeah."

"Cool. Okay then, here we go…"

Half an hour later Clyde was back in the console room listening to the chorus he'd just tracked. Besides the producer Sylicon Smoov, there was also his engineering assistant Raw D-Eel and two other guys who were just hanging out. Clyde didn't remember their names.

"So check it out," Smoov said, his finger hovering above a button on the mixing console. "Right here you sort of wander off. Like, you *thinking* instead of just singing."

He tapped the button. Clyde heard his voice falter right when it was supposed to rise and hold a bold expressive note. He nodded. "Yeah, I see that."

"Good," Smoov said. "Long as you get the message, we can dial it in the next time around."

"Yeah. You want me to try it now?"

"Not just yet, no. We got other parts to go over. Like here, right at the end, what you think about this?"

Sylicon played the very final moments of the song where after two cycles of the chorus, Clyde alternated between a firm, staccato rap and uttering goofy animal noises. The room burst out laughing.

When Clyde pulled his face out of his hands, he saw Sylicon raise his eyebrows and say, "So, whatchu think?"

"Man, I don't know," Clyde said. "It all sound kind of stupid, you know?"

"Stupid how? Your performance or the words themselves?"

"Both? Like, the rap part makes sense. I like the lyrics—he *feelin'* good in that moment. So why he now want to sound like a cow or a monkey?"

One of the guys who was sitting in touched his friend on the arm and said, "See, the kid don't get it yet. He don't *know!*"

Clyde blushed. All these guys were older. This was their crew, their studio, their song. Reeling from his own recent dud, he had accepted their invitation to come to the Bronx and get a coveted "featuring" credit on Sylicon Smoov's new single. But now he just felt dumb and out of his league.

He said quietly, "What don't I get?"

Sylicon took a puff from the blunt that Raw had just lit, then offered it to Clyde as he said, "It's like this. The cat in the song feels like a king. You know, he just tapped that hot piece of ass. But now this girl also in his head, because she drugged him with that Ho'Spice. She gave him some sex, but that was only the hook! One taste of that high and now he got to get more. 'Cause it be killin' him already!"

Clyde felt a rush through his eyes and head. He passed the blunt off. "So," he said, "it's like he kind of got tricked. But… why you want to say that in a song with your name on it?"

"For one," Sylicon said with a smirk, "because it's true. That's what happens with these bitches."

"You'd think the famous DJC would figure the other part," Raw D-Eel added.

"Help me out," Clyde said.

"Before we do," Smoov said, "you ain't a virgin, right? Or gay?"

"Nah, man! What the hell?"

The group laughed at Clyde's defensive plea. The blunt made its way around the room.

Smoov flashed his silver-and-purple grill into a smile. "Because, young man, every girl that listen to this song think that *she* gonna be the one to do that to you."

"Get ready!" the two friends called out, bringing balled fists up to their mouths and rolling around in their seats.

"Yeah," Smoov chuckled. "This ain't gonna flow only to me. You on this track too, son. Hos gon' be sniffin' you out, lookin' to reel you in. Break yo' heart and take yo' money!"

Clyde shook his head firmly. "Nope. I'm doin' music. Ain't going to fall in love. I got places to go."

"Love? Shit! I'm talkin' about babies. That's the *real* message in the song. Knock a bitch up, then watch how quick your royalties become *her* priority for twenty years."

Clyde reached for a crinkled sheet of paper that was on the console. "Let me look at this again. Hmm. No… I don't see anything at all talkin' about baby mama or whatever."

"Don't trouble yourself." Sylicon took the lyric sheet back into his hand. "Your job is to sing the words, get paid."

One of the guests tilted his head back and blew a thick stream up smoke upward. He said, "Just rap… and then wrap it up."

After a dead moment, the studio exploded in laughter.

"Ain't that the truth, though," Sylicon said. "DJC here talk about Reparations. *We* payin' Reparations just for doin' what come natural."

"Lie down with dogs, pay for puppies," the guy holding the blunt said.

"All them baby bills," Raw said, shaking his head. "World sees us put on them gold chains for the pictures, but it's the pink and blue chains that keep us hustlin' day and night!"

Smoov pointed a finger at Raw. "You know it. They jump into the sheets with you, no problem. Then, what? Here come they lawyer handin' you a whole other kind of spreadsheet."

There was a low rumble of agreement from the assembled crew.

Clyde said, "Y'all speakin' some real truth right now. Why not make a song 'bout all that?"

"That's *too* much truth," Smoov muttered. "No one really want to hear that."

"I did it," Clyde offered, folding his arms in self-satisfaction.

"Shit, kid," Raw said. "That's a one-off! A fluke. Go on, do it again. In fact, try and make a career always kicking over everybody's cup. I dare you."

Smoov waved his arm. "Come on, lay off the boy. He got pipes and a silver tongue. Long as he help us move this single, I say let him think whatever he wants."

Clyde nodded his head. "Come on then," he said, "give me another drag of that."

As Clyde closed his eyes, exhaling the weed out through his nostrils, Smoov said sternly, "Don't get too comfy now. You got to get back in there and make it right."

"No doubt. I'll deliver the goods."

Smoov thumped a fist into his open palm several times. "This is the hit factory, straight up! We can't be stopped. No, sir!"

"Never stop," Raw said lazily. "Not with all them mouths to feed…"

8. DREADFUL SILENCE

Chris Donohugh sat in the hazy late afternoon light of his Brooklyn apartment. He had Kate's home laptop open in front of him on the dining room table. A small black plastic device was dancing between his fingertips.

After a moment, the login screen appeared and he typed in Kate's password: ilovechrisd. Despite making a career in technology, Chris had never been able to convince her to add a number or capital letter to her passwords in all these years.

He disabled the computer's internet connection and then opened the program Kate used to check her work emails remotely. After poking around the various account settings, Chris scratched a few notes onto a pad and then turned his attention to the little black device.

He tapped around its tiny keypad, glancing briefly at his notes, then inserted the connector into a laptop port. The device's tiny screen lit up to full brightness and said, "Pairing… Searching… Authenticating… Embedding… Complete."

Chris removed the device and put it into his shirt breast pocket. He closed the email program, turned the internet back on, then quickly scanned the computer screen to make sure nothing else had accidentally opened or been changed. He pushed the top closed.

What the hell am I doing?

Chris returned Kate's laptop to the charger on the floor near the TV in the living room. He patted the pocket while making his way toward his office in the spare bedroom. The two Corgis followed slowly, their nails tapping against the hardwood floor as they trudged down the hallway.

Just as he was about to sit down in front of his own computer, out of the corner of his eye Chris caught sight of the little shrine dedicated to his old band Raucous Voice. Now relegated to a corner of a bookcase's lower shelf, this collection of mementos included their two 7" EPs, a shattered guitar's headstock that had been autographed by the band, and several small framed group photos.

Chris picked up one of the pictures. It had been taken outside a bar after one of their shows. He, singer Glenn Murray, and the two other guys were lined up in a happy drunken pose. He studied the faces—so young, so hopeful—and got a sick feeling. He sensed a vague regret that wouldn't come into focus. Or nostalgia for something that had been lost.

He stared into Glenn's eyes. Years had passed since that night, but their bond was so strong that Chris was now willing to use his own wife to spy on the HRA. Or maybe, Chris wondered, it was simply his own creeping doubts that had led him to this moment.

Stress after stress had hounded him all year, from Kate's medical battle to all the drama surrounding the HRA hack. And just when some semblance of normalcy began to return after the president's re-election, Kate was called down to Washington to meet with the Jeffries-Lao team.

Now Chris was left by himself to speculate on where this roller coaster ride would hurtle next. And he couldn't help but feel that the course of events was being influenced, if not guided, by Kate herself.

Her needs. Her existential crisis. Her career. Her suddenly relevant biological clock. And perhaps her relocating to the DC area to work for the president.

In moments like this, Chris felt more like a passenger than a partner. He was expected to both *give* what Kate needed, and *give in* to what she wanted. Meanwhile, all he felt he had to show for himself were the memories of a punk band that made about eight dollars a year in royalties from some European streaming service.

Chris returned the picture frame to the shelf after carefully dusting off the edges with his finger. He shuffled to the desk and sat down in the swivel chair. He connected the little black device to his computer. As his fingers entered the commands that would duplicate Kate's emails to the catch-all program on his system, Chris felt his head start to swim.

Suddenly he realized what it was he had been yearning for when thinking back on his band years. It wasn't about the time that had passed, or even the dreams of fame that never materialized. It was the loss of that energetic blind faith that had fueled them to write manic, politically charged anthems, then pile into a van and play shows at grimy clubs all across the Mid-Atlantic region.

That fire had slowly, almost stealthily died out while Chris went about the routine business of life in the adult world. Before, there had always been something to look forward to. But now in the silence of so many forgotten days, Chris saw the stark truth: The world he was meant to live in—where he could thrive and shine—was gone and possibly never to be seen again.

Instead, Chris found himself violating his wife's trust while she was meeting with the leader of the free world.

He felt so petty and lost. A small creature that had been led astray, perhaps since birth. Here was Kate standing on the precipice of professional glory, while he sat alone in near-darkness tinkering with hacker software. Chris had no idea how all the years of his life had drained into this paralyzing moment.

Panicking, he ran out of the room and grabbed his heavy coat. But just as he reached for the house keys, the wet bar came into view—and a giant bottle of cheap whiskey offered him its tantalizing curves.

An hour later, Chris was sitting on the floor of his office still wearing the coat. The record player he'd fished out of the closet was blaring a fast-moving punk rock track, the yellow splatter-vinyl spinning at 45 RPM. Chris took a pull out of the whiskey bottle, then pushed the fur-fringed hood away from his face.

He nodded in time with the song, suddenly sitting up in anticipation before shouting along with the chorus. "We know! ... Let's go! ... Gutter war! ... Explode!"

Chris fell back against the wall. He pumped his fist when the screaming guitar solo came in. "Hell yeah!" he applauded. "Raucous in the house!"

One of the Corgis started howling and jabbed its paws into Chris's leg. "You know it, pup!" he said, making a clumsy playful grab at the dog's ear.

Chris heard the house phone ring. The automated

voice announced, "Call from… *Kate*."

"Oh, shit," he blurted. He lifted the needle off the turntable and crawled across the floor out into the hallway. He picked up the receiver. "Hello?"

"Hi, Chrissy Poo!" Kate said. "I thought you'd be home. Whatcha doin'?"

Chris slipped out of the winter coat. "Hanging out with the pups. You know, uh… just listening to music, laying low."

"That doesn't sound too bad."

"Well, what about you? How'd it go?"

"As we speak," Kate said, "I'm riding in the back of a Towncar headed to my parents' place. Because we're going to *celebrate!*"

Chris flipped on the hall light and squinted. "Um… yeah? What happened?"

Kate's voice was beaming. "Today I hung out with Eileen! I also met Tony, Danielle, Natalie, all the insider peeps."

"Yeah? That's awesome."

"I couldn't believe how welcoming they all were. *Annnd…* they want me to work as a direct liaison between the HRA and the White House as they roll out sister offices in some of the smaller former colonies."

Chris licked his lips. He said, "Do you know *where* you'll be working?"

"We haven't figured out all those details yet. But hey! Can't you say 'congratulations'? Be *happy* for me, please."

"Oh, yeah," Chris mumbled. "That's amazing. But I guess maybe we thought that might happen, right?"

Kate was silent for a moment. "Chris. Have you been drinking?"

He exhaled audibly into the phone.

"Really?!" she said.

"I'm just having a couple beers."

"Hmm. Well, just don't forget to walk the critters, please."

"Sure, of course."

"I'm gonna get going now, Chris. Don't celebrate too hard without me."

"Ha, yeah. Tell your parents I say hi."

"Sure. 'Night!"

Twenty minutes later Chris was again wearing his coat, but now standing at a nearby street corner while the Corgis sniffed around the base of a stop sign. His stomach was a tight churning pit, and he looked searchingly at each person who walked past.

He scooped up the dogs' business and dropped the bag into a trash can on the way back to the apartment building. But he paused near the front steps, reluctant to go in. Because he knew what came next. The climb up the stairs while the dogs tugged at their leashes. Then passing into the dreadful silence that lay behind the front door.

No amount of music or alcohol could dull how profoundly alone Chris Donohugh felt tonight. And he simply could not be happy for Kate right now, not when feeling so little hope within himself.

9. WHO COULD REFUSE?

Kate Donohugh set down her things and eased into a chair at Reagan-National Airport. The bright morning sun of this clear day defied the cold air outside and warmed her face ever so slightly.

She sipped her to-go coffee and closed her eyes for a moment. During the early rush from her parents' house in nearby Arlington, Kate had just enough energy to get from their door all the way through check-in and security. But now that she was settled with a forty-five-minute wait until her flight home to New York boarded, the whirlwind of the last day suddenly caught up to her.

The quick trip down to DC. The private car picking her up VIP-style and driving directly to the White House. The dizzying encounter with all the president's men and women. Their joyful buzz and the promise of things to come for Kate. And finally a night out in Old Town Alexandria celebrating with her mother and father.

Now, as Kate blinked into the sunlight through the airport's giant window panes, that last pour of red wine was taking its toll. She pulled a pen out of her purse and turned her attention to a crossword puzzle. She sighed after a frustrated moment, using the pen more as a drumstick against the folded newspaper than actually filling in any of the little squares.

I'm never good at finishing these things.

Out of the corner of her right eye, she sensed that someone was staring at her. It was a woman, maybe a bit older than Kate. Now leaning away, whispering to someone else. Was she pointing at her too?

Kate couldn't stand the growing tension any longer and whipped her head around. The woman, who was sitting several seats down on the row facing her own, perked up and smiled. She then turned to a girl seated to her left, patted her on the back and made an encouraging gesture.

The ten-year-old child stood up and slowly approached. Kate realized she was clenching her coffee cup so hard that the thick cardboard was nearly buckling.

The girl stopped a few feet away. "Hi," she said nervously. "Are you… Kate?"

"I am indeed." Kate felt the pressure inside her body fall away. She exhaled, then said in a sweet tone, "And who are you?"

"Samantha." She looked back at the other woman and gave a thumbs up. "That's my mom."

Kate beckoned the woman to join them with a wave.

"Hi, I'm Meredith. I hope we're not disturbing you."

"No," Kate said, "not at all."

"We both recognized you and, I guess, did a double take since it was here in DC."

"Well, the HRA likes to fly us around."

"I'll bet. Um… Samantha here is just such a big fan of yours and wanted to say hi."

"Of me?" Kate blushed. "I haven't done anything—in public at least—to warrant that kind of praise, I don't think."

"*Someone* disagrees. Go on, Sam, tell her."

The girl smiled. "Ever since you were on *DDM TV*, I've been learning all about you. I even watched the show you did with Tina way back when."

"Wow," Kate said. "I'm impressed. And? What do you think?"

"That you're great!" Samantha raised her hand and waited until Kate gave her a high-five.

Meredith sat down beside Kate and confided, "Girls need more role models like you. Confident, involved… and strong enough to get up off the mat when life knocks you down."

Kate smiled. "Thank you, again. That's too kind."

"So tell us, what brought you down to the city?"

"Actually…"

Kate paused, then thought better of the momentary burst of pride that made her want to share everything about her day at the White House. "Oh, you know," she said, "just more of the endless training and meetings we have to endure."

"Of course," Meredith said. "And I can relate. I work with regulatory groups. Well, Samantha. I think we've taken up enough of Kate's time. Please say goodbye and wish her a safe flight."

The girl leaned in and gave Kate a hug. "Yay, Kate Donohugh!" she beamed. "La, la, la…"

Kate felt a bit flushed as she watched Sam skip away and start digging into her bright backpack.

"Bye now," Meredith said.

"Cheers," Kate said with a wave.

She tried to focus on the crossword again, but her mind was fluttering. *Role model?* Kate couldn't quite believe it. But seeing the smile on that girl's face gave Kate a kind of satisfaction that was far different than when assisting Beneficiaries or doing charity work.

Kate suddenly saw a new horizon open up where she might be a mentor, or even one day a leader of some kind. She thought about this White House opportunity and wondered if it could vault her toward that more quickly. Or perhaps it might hold her back?

She would discuss it all in depth with Chris. The truth was that there were a lot of things the two of them would need to lay out on the table soon. Deep down Kate knew that accepting an out-of-town job without fully consulting one's spouse wasn't a good look. The worst thing she could do was pack her bags without making some sort of maintenance plan for their relationship.

Because once again she was asking Chris to accept something big on her behalf. And whereas her illness and the HRA hack were life events they'd both had to react to, this new job was something… *important*. He would be *expected* to acquiesce—or else be seen as the bad guy.

Although, Kate figured that if Chris really pressed her about how much time she anticipated being away from home, she could always plead powerlessness. Because who could refuse when the President of the United States said jump?

An attendant at the podium announced that the New York flight was about to board. Kate gathered her things, gave Meredith and Samantha a final wave, then made her way directly to the front of the line for first-class boarding.

Flying at the president's behest did come with its perks.

10. BROADER IMPLICATIONS

A lanky young man approached the long folding table at the front of the meeting room. He picked up a thick hardcover from the mess of books and thumped it loudly against the surface.

"Alright, everybody," he said. "Let's take our seats and come to order."

Several dozen young adults separated from the groups they were standing in and filled the rows of folding chairs arranged near the table. A woman who had been conversing near the back of the room now joined the man up front. She set a briefcase down and smiled.

The man said, "This will be the first official meeting using our new name, the B&D Alliance. The change comes in deference to a request made by one of our newest members, who—while touched that we admire his bravery—prefers for the focus not to be about him. Thank you for everything, Luis."

People gave polite applause as the man turned to his left and bowed to Luis Ortega, who was seated in the front row. Luis nodded and mouthed, "Thank you." A girl seated to his right smiled, briefly laying her head on his shoulder.

"Now," the speaker said, "it's time for us to get to work. Joining me today is Sabine Plotz, an attorney specializing in immigration law. In recent years she has worked a variety of cases related to the HRA. Hopefully she can provide the legal insights we need to achieve our goals. Sabine?"

The woman, in her late thirties with long brown hair pulled back into a ponytail, and wearing a purple chambray skirt suit and maroon heels, shook hands.

"Thank you, Miguel," she said. She waved her hand over the table. "Somewhere within these volumes, we just might find the solution you desire. To turn the one-time, explicitly defined DDM deferral as pioneered by Mr. Ortega"—she tilted her head respectfully—"into a permanent exemption with broader implications. But the first question I must pose to this group is, what are you truly willing to give up in order to get your way?"

After a pause, someone in the crowd said, "We just want to be left alone."

"Believe me," the lawyer responded, "I understand what you mean. But the law always makes things more complicated than… black and white." She shrugged her shoulders. "Anyway, what I'm getting at is, despite the number of other Reparations-related court cases, there is no precedent for what you seek."

Miguel took a step forward, "Guys and gals, I think Ms. Plotz wants clarification—or better yet, a commitment about how far we're ready to take this thing."

"All the way!" someone else shouted.

Sabine tapped her toe against the floor three times. "Oh yeah? As in," she said skeptically, "complete renunciation of all HRA benefits? Or possibly going *all the way* to the Supreme Court?"

Three people in back—all Minoricans of different shades—clapped their hands in unison and said, "Leave us... alone! We want... to stay home!"

They sat down after several recitations of the chant.

Sabine began a slow wide arc around the table. She said, "I feel your passion, truly. You'd be surprised to read about the various legal challenges that have been brought by both Beneficiaries and Debtors over the past few years. My main concern today is that people are often not prepared for how *long* this process can take. You could wait *years* for your case to wind its way through the system—and possibly to only in the end not get what you want. Ask yourselves if you're *really* prepared to give up so much of your time in court or poring over documents, when the pain of a DDM assignment might be the quicker approach."

A college-aged female Cauc stood up. "Hi," she said. "My name is Lauren. I'm a pre-law student at Texas Tech trying to help out this group of young activists as best I can. Ms. Plotz, isn't it true that once these Beneficiaries formally begin the process, that they would be granted a temporary stay against any DDM call-ups?"

"That's correct," Sabine said. "But it wouldn't cancel the assignment altogether. Whenever your case is decided down the road, if you lose then that's it. Your obligation begins immediately thereafter. And if I know anything about life, it's a truism that one's future is always *busier* than today. Having done this professionally for years, I'm suggesting out of caution that the expedient option is to just bite the bullet."

Miguel turned to her and said, "Since we all value your time, I'm going to get to perhaps the biggest point, or strategy, of all. We *hope* that any legal proceedings take a long time."

"You do? Really?" The attorney seemed perplexed.

"Yes, because we intend our cases to outlast the Reparations program. And then it'll all just go away."

"Let me get this straight. As in, you envision not just winning an exemption for yourselves, but for the entire HRA to cease operations?"

Members of the group began to cheer.

Sabine leaned forward onto the end of the table and shook her head. She said slowly, "Okay, there's a lot to think about here. First, do you know how hard it is to repeal just the average local law? That becomes almost impossible when you're dealing with a national administration like the HRA. Why? Because too many interwoven special interests act as a root system to keep it entrenched."

"Too many barnacles!" a man yelled. "Sink the whole thing!"

"Believe me, I'm not defending how it all operates. Now," Plotz said, staring intently at the group, "there's also the issue of... well, I don't know if the word is perspective, or something else. But you all are so young. You never experienced any of the privation and cruelty which the Reparations program sought to make amends for. I'm sure that many people would say you're being ungrateful, just because your lives might be inconvenienced. Tell me, how many of your ancestral homelands have a military draft, for instance?"

"Hey, I thought you were supposed to be advocating *for* us," the same man called out.

"And I am," the lawyer said. "Which includes using my real-world experience to make you aware of the obstacles such a campaign might run into."

As the gathering started to murmur to one another, the young pre-law student stood up again. She said, "Ms. Plotz, if I may add, since you're meeting us all for the first time. This is a very brave and committed group fighting for their rights as they see fit. They have so many wonderful hopes and dreams that might go from delayed to bottled up forever, if the government is allowed to exert so much power over their lives."

A few whistles came in response.

Sabine said, "Lauren, thank for you helping me to understand. If you all are absolutely set on seeing this through to the end... Well, I've fulfilled my responsibility to inform you about the road ahead, so it appears we're ready to formally proceed." She gave a hearty smile. "The HRA better watch out, because here we come!"

Everybody stood up and applauded. Some left their seats and crowded around Sabine and Miguel.

Luis Ortega sat blinking through his glasses, bewildered about the turn of events that had plucked him out of obscurity and seemed unwilling to let go.

He felt Cristina slide her arm through his own. She smiled up at him. He playfully scratched the top of her head with his free hand.

This burgeoning movement that was trying to defeat the HRA's DDM program had all started because Luis just wanted to make his family proud as a college student. Then these people here at the meeting had brought a very special girl into his life.

He didn't fear what came next as long as Cristina stayed by his side.

11. ONE OF US

The hood was finally yanked off his head. It had remained in place from the moment he was first thrown inside a van, then hustled with claws digging into his back to a prop plane, until finally being driven to this unknown location several miles from the airport.

Marcus Young squinted in the searing fluorescent light. He felt someone jam a water bottle into one of his zip-tied hands.

"Here," a voice behind him said. "Drink up."

Marcus knew better than to try turning around to see who was in the room with him. The scenery had quickly confirmed his suspicion that he was in a law enforcement interrogation room. The only question was who had taken him into custody—DHS, HRA, or his own employer, the FBI?

He kept his head bowed and unscrewed the bottle cap. He drank half of the water in several gulps, then waited for the other man to speak again.

Hands pressed down onto his shoulders.

"Marcus, Marcus, Marcus… what *ever* are we going

to do with you?"

The man released his grip and stepped forward, leaning a hip against the table that was in front of Marcus.

"Well…. what do you have to say for yourself?"

Marcus felt the man staring at his drooping face. Slowly he looked up and said, "If I knew who you were —who you worked for—I could give you a better answer."

"Ha! Who do I *work for?* The same as you. Until recently, that is."

Marcus nodded. "Mm. I figured as much. That you'd track me down sooner or later."

"Yup. But I gotta hand it to you. You took the concept of 'embedding a field agent' to a whole new level. If you knew the lengths we went to, to track you down…"

"Enough with the theatrics, please." Marcus nodded his head at the security cameras and the two-way mirror that was in the wall directly across from him. "I'm not scared. You won't have to *beat it* out of me. And besides, I'm still one of you guys."

The other man, who was wearing a hybrid business-tactical suit made of strong woven synthetic material, now reached into one of the half-dozen cargo pockets and removed a porcelain cigar. He sat in a chair and put his feet up on the table.

"One of us, eh?" he said, blowing a cloud of shimmering synth-smoke into the air. "Federal Bureau of Investigation… or was that, in your case, Indoctrination? Mod bless you—am I right?"

Marcus didn't react to the smirk that followed this jab. He gave a slight shrug, then said, "I'll interpret this as just part of your power play, and not an example of religious persecution. So why not extend a little professional courtesy my way? You'll probably get what you want a lot easier."

A thoughtful expression replaced the interrogator's grin. "Okay," he said, chewing several times. "Special Agent Young, my name's Axelsson. *Supervisory Special Agent* Axelsson. And it was my team, in fact, that received all your info drops from inside the Mall. For most of those six months you were doing excellent work. I even recall once or twice telling the guys that someday I hoped to meet you. Can ya believe that?"

Axelsson cocked an eyebrow, then chomped down on the faux-cigar's rubber tip.

Marcus said, "And what was your takeaway from my reports?"

"Oh… Mostly harmless, the Modestians themselves. But I'm not so certain about the higher-ups…"

"Sir, I assure you that—"

"Please," Axelsson said with a wave. "I think your opinion might be a little biased."

"But you don't intend to take any action against them, do you? They've done nothing wrong!"

"Calm yourself, Mr. Young. This isn't about *them* anyway. The reason we're here today is because of you! You goddamn deserter!"

Marcus couldn't help but flinch when Axelsson's hand came slamming down onto the metal tabletop. He sensed his newfound Modestian serenity grappling with the old adrenaline-fueled habits of his life in the FBI. He exhaled coolly.

"SSA Axelsson," he said, "you took me away from a most meaningful task out on the Farm. I can't even imagine the chaos and worry that your raid inflicted upon everyone there. And when word gets back to the church… Just tell me, was anyone hurt?"

"No, no," Axelsson said. "We left them all in peace.

Even the Debtor whose fugitive status came up during the retinal scans. *You* were the target."

"Well… I thank you for leaving them be. Those men are all military vets. Served their country, *the same as you*. Now, what the hell do you want from me?"

Axelsson stood up with a laugh, throwing out his arms as he walked toward the mirror and said, "He thinks he's running this thing! Who knows, maybe that's just one of the mind-controlling tricks he learned from that cult."

The man swiveled back toward Marcus, saying, "I don't know how much news you've been privy to since you disappeared two weeks ago. But our law enforcement brothers have been kickin' ass lately. Rounding up Sentinels of Jubilee members high and low, all over the country."

"I'd heard a bit," Marcus said. "But what does that have to do with me?"

"Special Agent Young, you don't even recognize an olive branch when it's being waved in front of your face, do you?"

"I still don't understand."

"Jesus Christ!" Axelsson pleaded. "Think about it, will ya? I could have you disappeared into solitary if I really wanted to bust your balls. But you did some admirable work living among those Modestians, and so we're willing to overlook your lapse of conduct for the moment—because we need you back out in the field to land us a big fish."

Marcus reflected briefly, then said, "Assuming I succeed, what happens to me after you double back around?"

Axelsson pointed his cigar at Marcus. "Do you, uh, really trust this guy, the Prescient One?"

Marcus hesitated, not wanting to reveal that he had

spoken intimately with the church leader once before—
let alone that he knew the man's treasonous secret. He
said, "His Prescience may come across as an enigma,
or eccentric, but his motives are pure. As are his
methods. I see no reason to suspect anything nefarious
or perverted about him."

"And you," Axelsson continued probing, "you're so
smitten with this religion that you would continue on as
a believer?"

"With Mod as my witness."

"Fine. I'm sure we'll find some way to
accommodate this... unique situation. How lucky for
you that you're such an effective agent."

"What's my new assignment?" Marcus asked.

SSA Axelsson made a beckoning motion in the
mirror. Seconds later another man wearing a traditional
business suit entered, then handed over an accordion
folder before departing. Axelsson carefully laid out a
number of documents on the table.

"Here," he said, "are three regions of the country
that suffered a spate of SOJ-related sabotage in the past
five months."

"*Five?*" Marcus said, puzzled. "I thought these guys
had been moving silently until that first hack. Which
was when, early October?"

"Correct. But they were active long before anyone
even knew of their existence. Only now have we been
able to piece together events that just seemed like
random acts of vandalism."

"I see. So what am I looking at here with these
particular areas? From the maps it looks like Boston,
Metro New York, and parts of Michigan."

"Right again," Axelsson said. He held up a grainy
black-and-white photograph of a bearded man who
seemed poised to devour a microphone clasped in his
fist. "Do you know who this is?"

Marcus shook his head. "I have no idea. Should I?"

Axelsson dropped the picture onto the other papers. "No," he said. "Just the lead singer of a band no one ever heard of. But! This band, which calls itself Bleeding the Aggregate, just so happens to have been out on the road playing at dive bars the exact same dates these crimes were committed."

Marcus began to speak, then held up his joined hands. "Could you untie me, please?"

"Of course." Axelsson split the zip-tie with a small knife he produced from a cargo pocket.

"Okay," Marcus said, rubbing his wrists before taking up some of the papers. "First of all, I see gaps between these events. Couple of weeks here. And over a month between Detroit and Boston. What gives?"

"That's because these were individual mini-tours. Like I said, this is not a famous band. Members are in their thirties, work regular day jobs. Anyhow, we're confident these trips were booked as cover so that this man with the beard could go out and coordinate with other Sentinels between shows."

"If true, that's quite clever." Marcus tapped the photograph with his finger. "So tell me, who is this guy?"

"His name is Glenn Murray. Originally from Maine, currently lives in the Philadelphia area. Works off and on doing industrial paint contracting."

"So if you know where he lives, and everyone else is getting arrested right now, why not just take him in?"

"Because," Axelsson said, leaning onto the table with a grin, "Bleeding the Aggregate has a handful of shows booked starting next weekend. And I want you, Special Agent Young, to lead the team that catches Mr. Murray and his Sentinel conspirators in the act."

"Where?"

"First stop, Washington, DC."

12. ALL THEM FUNERALS

"What about them lyrics Smooth Move made you sing?" Dawna Jenkins asked, adjusting herself on the kitchen stool.

"Who? You mean Sylicon Smoov?"

"Whateva he call himself. Point is, sound like he got a rough crew over there."

"Nah." Clyde gave a sour wave. "He teachin' me the ropes. What it take to be a successful producer. Like he said, 'Great beats keep you from sleepin' on the streets.' "

Ms. Jenkins laughed. "Listen to yourself. For how many weeks and months did you go on about how 'I gotta be my own artist, can't sell out'? Sure sound like you changed your tune."

"But this is different. That dude Pryor, he shifty, sneaky like. Meanwhile Mr. Smoov, he treat me with respect like a brother does. Yeah, Pryor took me out to dinner and stuff, but Smoov's crew, they know how to *chill*."

"Yeah, they chillin' while you drive them to the

bank. Black sellout's no different from a white sellout. Except…"

Clyde perked up. "Except what?"

Dawna got up and moved around the counter, wiping some invisible crumbs into her hands. "I doubt you gonna like what I think, or will even believe what I got to say."

"Come on, Mama," Clyde said. "Try me."

"Aight, then." She stepped back and leaned against the sink. "There's other differences between Mr. Pryor and your friend Smoov. Those boys he run with all got criminal records. Some of it real nasty, not just for the petty stuff."

"But Octavius—"

"Shush! And don't you ever, *ever* say such a thing in this house again. Lord have mercy on this boy and his mouth. Clyde, my son. Just 'cause you ain't a nobody no more, and got a real focus in your life, that don't make your world any less dangerous."

"I know, I know…" Clyde started pacing in the kitchen. He said, "But I won't sing any stuff about gang bangin' or robbin', I promise you."

Dawna threw up her hands. "Do you think the real criminals give a damn? All they know is you got fame, and that means money. So when they see you roll up to Mr. Smoov's spot, they see prey. And I *know* you ain't tough like… Mr. O., who can handle hisself. I wouldn't even want you to try."

"So what are you sayin'?" Clyde pleaded. "I got to make some kind of play. It ain't no fun to do stuff alone. Bad for your career, too."

"That's well and good. But since you don't play a real instrument like the violin, which would always keep you *safe*, I really think you should reconsider Eddie's offer."

Clyde paused for a moment. "You callin' him Eddie now, huh? You talk to that man?"

"Son, I just want what's best for you in the long run. And that don't only mean hits or money. I want you to *live* for a long time. So we got to find that place in the world where you can make the music that moves you, but you ain't in danger of being killed in some drive-by. Be such a waste…"

Dawna reached an arm forward and pulled Clyde in for a hug.

"Aw, thank you, Mama."

"I just love you too much. And I've seen enough pain in my lifetime already. Trips to the hospital, visits up at the jail. And all them funerals, my God…"

Clyde slowly let go. He wiped a tear from his cheek when his face was out of Dawna's line of sight. Just then he heard a few thumps on the carpeted stairs. His nephew Tyrell was in pajamas making his way down toward them.

"Hey, sleepy dude," Clyde said. "Have a nice nap?"

"Uh-huh."

Clyde knelt down on the bottom step. Tyrell jumped onto his back and yelled, "Yeah! Let's go!"

"Where to, kiddo?"

"Living room! I wanna watch TV."

"What, you don't wanna say hi to Gramma?"

Tyrell shook his head. "I already saw her this morning."

"That's harsh, though. If you be nice, I bet she'll make us a snack."

"Okay, we see her."

Clyde jerked around and made a whinnying noise as he galloped into the kitchen. "Snack time!" he yelled. "The horse and his rider are hungry. Whatchu got in here?"

Dawna kissed Tyrell on the head. "Hi, little man. Want Gramma to get you something?"

The boy looked around the room. "Popcorn," he said. "And ice cream!"

"Now, Tee," Dawna said, "we gonna have dinner not too long from now. Let's pick one of those. I think popcorn is a great idea. Maybe I'll have a few nibbles myself, in fact."

"Noooo! All for meeee!" Tyrell smiled. "Now giddy-up, horsey!"

Tyrell slapped Clyde on the shoulder and then they were off running into the front room.

Dawna poked around the cupboard and pulled out a bag of microwave popcorn. As the kernels slowly inflated the bag, she glanced in on the boys sitting together on the couch and smiled.

It was good to see them bonding. And safe. She intended to keep it that way.

13. FOREVER HOME

Matthias Witherspoon fell into step with the procession of men dressed in full-length cerulean blue tunics. A line of female Modestians wearing matching silver outfits kept pace along the other side of the corridor.

As they walked, Matthias could hear the hypnotic somber tones of an organ's low register. He found the occasional bright flourishes curious, noting that Modestian music was much more affecting on a primal level than the Christian hymns performed at his church back in Ohio.

Moments later the group entered a wide open area beneath triangular skylights. There was a round fountain in the middle, but for today the water had been turned off. Up front, ten rows of padded folding chairs faced a small stage that was decorated with enormous bouquets of pastel flowers and marble statues that were at the same time beautiful, demure, and striking.

As ushers led guests down the center aisle to their seats, Matthias noted that, as was often the case at the Mall of Absolution, the two genders sat separately.

However, he had been told by one of the excitable young novitiates he'd struck up a friendship with, that after the wedding vows had been taken, Modestians were known to loosen their collars with pagan abandon.

The organ began to play more softly now. Matthias saw heads turn toward the aisle. He looked back just as a regal-looking man wearing a silk teal-and-silver striped robe strode past with firm, deliberate steps. This man was followed by two adolescent couples bearing small bouquets of ivory roses, who then took their places at the back of the stage.

A new, more bombastic musical arrangement filled the air. Again the guests turned their heads back.

Matthias, who had attended and officiated many weddings during his years as a preacher, was shocked when he saw not bridesmaids and groomsmen, or even family members, but a figure covered from head to toe by a large piece of shimmering blue cloth. Three young children were pulling this person forward on a small square cart using attached ropes.

The reverend was momentarily appalled, being unable to avoid seeing similarities between this spectacle and the humiliating atonement rituals he used to lead in debtors' prison yards. As the cloaked figure rolled slowly past, Matthias asked God both for strength and forgiveness.

Had he been fooled into visiting a lunatic asylum that was only masquerading as a church? He took wry solace in the fact that he would very soon find out the truth.

The little wagon stopped in front of the stage, then the children dropped the ropes onto the carpet and carefully guided the draped figure up the three steps and into position on the priest's left side.

As the music blended into a more serene aria, Matthias saw that yet another cart was on its way. He felt perspiration begin to form on his temples as the next arrival, similarly cloaked in silver, was wheeled down the aisle. Resisting the instinct to cross himself, Matthias instead fished around under his clumsy garment in search of a handkerchief to dab his face.

This obscured individual was escorted into place beside the priest, who himself then took a step forward and spread his arms wide.

"Mod be with you," he said.

"And also with you," the seated guests replied. "Amen."

I know that one at least, Matthias thought.

"Let us rejoice," the priest said, "for today is one of the great moments in Modestian life. The joining together of two souls under the banner of our still very young religion. This old tradition that, whether through neglect or sullied institutions, seems to have fallen out of favor in the wider world. But today we revitalize it within the Church of Modestianity."

The man turned to the first figure and placed a palm upon its head. He said solemnly, "Brother Reese Carter. You came to us one year ago from a small town in Nebraska. Everything about you screamed for 'the new.' A new perspective for a world in flux. A new religion that had the courage and zest to truly *live*, and not hide behind rote doctrine. And ultimately, you sought a new type of woman to be your bride."

Suddenly the priest yanked the cloth up and tossed it away. Matthias saw a handsome white man who was not a day over twenty-five. He stood proudly in an electrifying blue tuxedo, a lightning rod of confidence and vitality from head to toe.

The groom and the priest exchanged a warm smile.

Then the official swung slowly around and placed a hand upon the other covered head.

"Sister Ramona," he said, "precious jewel of the Bell family, who all made their way to this Modestian sanctuary from rural Utah ten months ago. You confided in me that your clan is a bit restless when it comes to churches, but I hope today's ceremony means that you personally *have* found a forever home with us."

The priest quickly disposed of the silver fabric, which revealed to all an angelic brunette whose cheeks sparkled with glitter. She smiled at the priest, who now turned to face the crowd.

"Let us praise Mod and the Prescient One for bringing together these two yearning souls…"

As the official spoke about the young couple's first meeting and carefully supervised courtship, Matthias instead found himself thinking about the Prescient One. For the reverend had lived within these church walls for nearly a week, but still had not gotten an audience with the Modestian founder and leader.

He had *seen* him speak at one of the larger community gatherings, but any inquiry about their previously scheduled appointment was met with vague answers from the elders. And as much as Matthias was enjoying his sabbatical among these happy Modestians, he could not put off his own church responsibilities back home indefinitely.

"…and so I ask you, Brother Carter," the priest said, "do you willingly and joyfully accept the responsibilities of husband and eternal partner?"

The young man on stage inhaled deeply. "I do."

"And do you, Sister Bell," the priest said after pivoting to his right, "take this man as your protector and conscience? Whom you will serve and honor and provide with children?"

Ramona turned her head toward the wedding guests. Her eyes scanned across the dozens of eager faces. Finally she looked into Reese's eyes and gave a firm, contended nod. "I do."

Smiling brightly, the priest said with great emotion, "As you embark upon your new life as one, I offer this personal bit of advice. If you play to your strengths and always remember to lean on each other, you will find the stamina to thrive in the decades to come. Now, I am elated to declare you husband and wife. Sir, you may kiss your bride!"

Matthias felt his throat catch as he watched the young couple intertwine their fingers before slowly leaning in. Maintaining eye contact, Reese and Ramona sealed their union with a delicate but long-lasting kiss.

Reverend Witherspoon now found himself almost unable to breathe. A tear ran down his cheek. He saw the man next to him bare his teeth in a satisfied smile, which somehow caused all of his own tension to release.

Matthias exhaled slowly and deeply, sensing in his mind's eye a flicker of his own wedding day many years ago. Where it had all gone wrong with Janelle he didn't have the heart to wonder about, not now during such a hopeful and touching moment.

He watched the newlyweds through misty eyes as they walked down the aisle together, their joined hands raised in triumph like sports champions. The young children who had earlier brought them in on the dollies now danced and frolicked in their wake.

The Reverend Matthias G. Witherspoon sat back and sighed. Whenever he thought he'd had enough of this eccentric church, he always experienced something new which awakened a corner of his heart that had gone dormant over the years. Whether those dead ends had manifested through neglect, ego, or cynicism did not matter now. He was thawing and finally tasting that rebirth which he had come here humbly seeking.

He also saw that he would be wise not to feel frustrated by the Prescient One's continued unavailability. "All in good time" was a message that every philosopher or religion worth its salt preached. Just as Matthias himself had advised parishioners in need of guidance a thousand times before.

Reverend Witherspoon would wait. He would live among these Modestians and learn from them everything that his own God had allotted for this interfaith experience.

And perhaps one day, Matthias mused, he would be known as… The *Patient* One.

14. TEMPTATION

Cornelius Alemán was standing with his back to the room while inspecting a row of antique books. He wore a beige linen blazer and rustic gray slacks, and his lush head of silver hair had been gelled into place. He turned around.

"Victor," he said, "so wonderful of you to come. Please, join me."

The elder gentleman motioned toward several brown leather seats and couches that were arrayed in a square in the middle of the lushly appointed living room. Drawn semi-opaque shades filtered the outside light, and several small lamps added a soft yellow glow.

Victor Dominguez, fresh off a charter flight at Alemán's expense, which was followed by a ride in a restored vintage car out to this secluded Vermont mansion, extended his hand.

"Pleased to meet you," Victor said. "Your estate is breathtaking."

"Thank you kindly," Cornelius said. *"Mi familia*

never understood why I would choose to live so far away from the border states. But then again, for some reason I have always loved the cold. Please, sit."

The men sat catty-cornered to one another in deep, plush leather chairs. A moment later, a middle-aged butler with bronze skin and shimmering black hair parted to the side entered the room.

"Bartolo," Alemán said, "I think we're ready."

"Excellent, sir." The butler approached, his shoes barely making a sound on the walnut flooring. "*Señor* Dominguez, would you care for something to drink?"

Victor consulted his watch. "Do you have sparkling water?"

"Of course. I will bring it immediately. And for you, Master Cornelius?"

The old man waved his hand. "The usual, with plenty of ice, please."

"Very good, gentlemen." Bartolo bowed his head and exited the room.

Cornelius smiled and rubbed his hands together gently. They were immense paws, but Victor had noticed during their initial greeting that these were more like soft pillows than a forceful weapon.

Alemán said, "Victor, I am so glad you agreed to meet with me. And before we begin, I do apologize for my outburst at the end of our first phone call."

Victor tilted his head, saying, "I honestly didn't know what to make of it."

"Sometimes I just get carried away." Cornelius smiled. "It's not what I really meant at all."

"I'm glad I made the trip then. To get a clarification."

"Think of it this way. I'm not a young man anymore, Victor. I turned seventy earlier this year."

"Congratulations."

"Yes, thank you," Alemán said. "When you've reached my age—and have *engaged* with life the whole time—you find that your *understanding* of things helps in overcoming all the fatigue you may feel in body and mind. Like any man who's honest with himself, I can admit that I've had more defeats than triumphs. But that doesn't mean now, just because my hair is gray, I am willing to quietly fade away."

Cornelius thumped the arm of his chair, then straightened his posture.

At that moment, the butler returned carrying a silver drink tray. He deftly slid a small table into the open space between the outside of the leather chairs, then placed two coasters down in one swift motion. Napkins bearing a coat of arms were also deposited, and finally Bartolo's white gloves reached for the drinks. A faint blue cylinder for Victor, and Cornelius received an oversize clear tumbler filled with amber liquid and three large pieces of ice. Bartolo withdrew without a word.

"Victor," Alemán said, as they brought the glasses together for a delicate clink, "I see tremendous leadership potential in you. Yes, sitting before me is a man who could unlock centuries of greatness."

"That's very flattering," Victor said. "I'm honored you would think that of me. But I'm still dressing my wounds right now, so in truth, I don't know how much fight I've got left at the moment."

"Don't worry about that." Cornelius patted Victor on the wrist. "Life proceeds in phases. There are periods of rest. Thought. And then, decisive action!"

"I hope that my story is just in an intermission then, and not over."

"Indeed, young man. Especially now that we're having this meeting of the minds. Tell me, does the name Luis Ortega mean anything to you?"

"Of course," Victor said. "He's the college kid who got the HRA to change several of its DDM rules."

"Yes, correct! People are referring to it sardonically as 'Bennies Choice.' What I find remarkable is that he was just a bit player at the time of the Sentinels' hack. In fact, if you'll remember, he was standing on stage while the masked man delivered his manifesto to the world. But it was *Luis* who ended up stirring an awakening among a segment of the population which the Sentinels could never dream of reaching."

"Beneficiaries," Victor said quietly.

"Yes! Empowering them to think for themselves through a spontaneous act of courage."

"No manifesto required."

Cornelius's eyes twinkled. "And that scares the daylights out of everyone from the White House on down. People whose lives revolve around making promises with strings attached."

"Ah." Dominguez pointed a finger skyward. "Because the 'hand up' often sets limits on how far you actually rise."

"It's no accident, Victor. If no one needs the HRA's assistance, not only will many highly educated people be out of a job, but perhaps a whole philosophy will also come into question."

"The missionary do-gooder." Victor was becoming more animated now. "I've been fighting an uphill battle against these types my whole adult life. They hide behind nice-sounding words, then call *you* taboo names to put you on the defensive if you disagree with their agenda."

"So true," Alemán said, taking a sip from his glass. "But look at what an average Jose was able to achieve. He put his foot down and moved the mountain that is the HRA."

Victor nodded and said, "He did more than that, actually. He put his body on the line. Luis could have been killed the way the FBI apprehended him."

"Yes," Cornelius conceded, "but the bigger point is that he never had the infrastructure or even an agenda like the SOJ did. But he sure made those bastards scramble!"

Victor paused. "So, what are you saying? Use him directly, or hold up his example to recruit other Davids to erode the HRA Goliath?"

"Here are the facts, *compadre*. As highly as we think of ourselves, we can't win this battle through leadership alone. We need the support of many Luis Ortega clones. Young, apolitical, family oriented... and sometimes not all that intelligent. Or at least, not likely to consider the big picture in the way that we do."

"Forgive me for saying this, Mr. Alemán, but it sounds like you're dreaming of a peasants' revolt. That has not gone well for our people in the past."

"Victor, please!" There was a fire in the old man's eyes. "Is that not what we're seeing among the Caucasians, who either support the SOJ or are disobeying the law in a hundred ways?"

"But the difference is," Victor said, "they *know* why they're angry. Latiz-Americans are the exact opposite. They're *glad* to be here. And in their heart of hearts, many of them know they caught a lucky break being granted amnesty in 'twenty-one. I think the last thing they want to do is make America reconsider its past generosity."

Cornelius shook his head. "But don't you see? It's too late! What this election showed is that we've crossed the tipping point. Not just demographically, but more importantly in terms of *participation*. The likes of

Luis Ortega may not know *why* they're voting for whom or what—but it only matters that we got them to the polls. Now let's get them to take action."

Victor was baffled. "And do what?"

"Whatever we want them to."

"Just like that? At the snap of your fingers?"

"Someone's, perhaps. But Senator, another truth about getting older and having many responsibilities is that whether you want to or not, you start to see the world *as it is*. And sadly, it is barely at all what you wish it to be. But with this clarity, at least you can, as in the style of the martial arts, use your surroundings and the existing momentum to bring the world closer to that more pleasant vision in your mind."

Victor shifted in his seat. He said, "Give me a concrete example, please."

"Certainly," Alemán said. "A person coming here from another country fifty years ago was required out of necessity to fit in. Learn the language, join their new community—and get to work. But in this century? It seems as if people only move to the United States for the running water and abundance of food. These new generations do not care about the First Amendment. And any interest they take in the country's history comes from a place of grievance—either to justify their own short-sighted gluttony, or to excuse their disdain for the virtues of civic life."

"Now wait," Victor said, feeling his head start to throb. "These are the same people you were just plotting to... I don't know... harness or inspire?"

"Yes indeed." Cornelius inhaled deeply. "Pardon me if I sound too cynical. I'm sure they're all good people with nieces and other beloved *familia*, but no one gets a pass in this life. No matter the color of your skin, where you came from, or how long ago you stepped off the boat. You have to *pay attention* if you don't want to be abused. Especially here in the busy United States—because this isn't the jungles of Guatemala, nor the dusty towns of our Mexican homeland.

"So these people," Alemán continued, "my cousins. They think they can sleepwalk forever. The train of ants that walked across the border, whose children speak English and even go to college—they still don't want to put it all together!"

Dominguez crumpled his napkin in frustration. "You're making *me* feel stupid now. Just what are you getting at? Because on the phone you had me thinking that your interest was in the people still living south of the border."

"Bear with me, please. If I can't wake Latizos up," Cornelius said, "I will at least corral them for my own purposes. Consider that they could have made history by electing you as the first Hispanic president. But so many of them were stuck looking backwards, caught up in the old narrative—because they lacked the integrity, *the individual courage* to renounce that Reparations check. Money which deep down most of them know they don't even deserve. And that, Senator, is the sickness I have vowed to prevent from spreading further south."

Victor looked down at his hands. "You think *they* are the reason why I lost the election?"

Cornelius leaned forward and brought a hand to his chin. He said, "It pains me to say this, believe me. But at their core they lack any sort of grand vision for the future. They're content to sit on their front porch and watch the neighborhood stagnate—they never think to climb the hill and contemplate the world beyond! But regardless, it is still out there and will be won by those who dare."

Victor Dominguez adjusted himself in the deep leather seat. "And you see that in me?"

Alemán smiled. "A tad reckless and unrefined… but yes, it is there within you, my friend."

"But perhaps I'm too set in my ways to cultivate? I'm no genius. And maybe not even a dyed-in-the-wool conservative. It's likely that I fell in with the pro-business side only by chance. All those days on the job site swapping out pipes with my father, and seeing him pinch pennies to provide for us. Did that give me a better chance of standing out, as opposed to being just another Minorican calling for more entitlements?"

"That could be part of it," Cornelius said. "But Victor, you carried us so close. Under the radar, all by yourself! I could never hope to achieve my goals, let alone so soon, without the bold charge you just made. Incredible… *salud!*"

Cornelius drained his whiskey, crunching a bit of ice as he set the glass down.

"I do appreciate this tribute," Victor said. "My ego hates to think that in some ways, it was just a convergence of factors much bigger than myself that put me in such a position."

"As if you were perhaps… sleepwalking?" The old man smiled. His gelled silver hair looked like grooved concrete in the afternoon's fading light.

"You seem to know me better than I do," Dominguez said.

"I just know life, Victor. Even if you only felt like a passenger, the day you realized that the party intended for you to lose, that's when you started throwing real punches. Lunging wildly, and not caring *who* you hit. It was beautiful!"

"Yes but, now that I've lost, my Senate colleagues are cold and often unavailable. People who in the final weeks of the campaign became very friendly when they smelled an upset. Now where are they?"

"But *I'm* here." Cornelius cupped his hands on top of his knees. "Sitting before you, face to face. *Hombre a hombre.*"

Victor exhaled, then clenched his jaw. "I am not so hurt as to go running into the arms of the next person who says that they approve of me. I too am old enough to endure defeat and disrespect."

"Of course." Alemán raised his palms in a placating gesture. "I'm not trying to scoop you up on the rebound. Here it is: this country is torn along many lines right now. The Dramacrats used to speak to Latizo interests, but our rising numbers and grinding work ethic reveal that we don't need their handouts anymore. Victor, the Left has chosen to be the party of the *loser*, even as they pat themselves on the back encouraging 'the underdog.' The Rebellicans, meanwhile, are in an eternal identity crisis. They too obsess over the past—but for them, instead of injustice, it's a perceived *greatness* that they allow to be chipped away for fear of... being spoken of unpleasantly. So, with such interparty weakness, do you finally understand why I see an opportunity?"

"You want to create a new third party?" Victor asked slowly.

"Yessss!"

"For Latizos? With me as the first leader?"

Cornelius smiled broadly. "The face, at least. You'll have a lot of backline support. From me, of course. And others. We will provide a road map so that it doesn't fall on its face out of the starting gate."

Victor Dominguez's eyes were wide in astonishment. "Do you really think it's easier to reach tens of millions of, as you say, sleepwalking Hispanics, rather than to end one faltering government program?"

"No. But it's more essential! To look *forward* with confidence. To not simply sit back complacently because your material needs are provided for—because that is the surest way to fall right back into dependence. After that, the helpless become the conquered. My friend, if Latizos are too sheepish to feel any sense of destiny after having spread across the United States, then I will *create* one for them!"

Cornelius Alemán stood up and shook his fist.

Senator Victor Dominguez sat very still in his chair while looking into the face of this impassioned man. He thought of his wife Jaclyn and their three children. He knew that he was now, suddenly, at a crossroads far greater than even that fateful moment when he first decided to run for president.

15. HEADS WILL ROLL

On the morning of November eighteenth, a viral video began to make the rounds on underground internet chat rooms. Within two days it had already been viewed fifteen million times. A group calling itself The Last Sentinel claimed responsibility.

The six-minute clip was titled "Explosive Forbidden Video Reveals Secret Government Pre-Education Camps for Children." Further details were provided in the description section:

"Watch as a masked team of Sentinels of Jubilee sympathizers infiltrate a South Carolina facility in this daring nighttime raid. It is here that an HRA-funded program houses and indoctrinates the children of imprisoned Debtors. Warning: The contents of this video will likely shock the sensibilities of any freedom-loving American."

The footage was compiled from cameras worn by several of the raiding party. They first moved briskly through a wooded area, before breaching the perimeter fence. They next surveyed four small structures before converging upon a small church house, whose bright lights and large windows revealed the scene inside.

Two dozen children ranging in age from three to ten, and whose faces were blurred out, chanted in unison with a woman wearing a bright green dress. Captioning provided with the video read, "The past is my burden, but the future starts with me. The ends justify the teams, because the friends multiply the dreams."

Next the raiders breached the windows and doors. Brandishing bats and Tasers, they quickly subdued the half-dozen staff members without inflicting violence, then tied them up. The children, who at first had begun to panic in the chaos, were soon calmed by the soothing voice of a masked woman.

A large banner above the teaching board read, "Everything is racist. Everything else is a human right."

After the building was secured, one of the team members removed his mask and fell to his knees as he embraced two of the children. The video clip ended here, with these final words appearing on the screen: "The Sentinels are reuniting families. Pledge your support so we can fight back against this out-of-control government."

President Eileen Jeffries-Lao turned away from the projection screen in disgust. The small group of staff members, who had already been working late at the White House, now sat in silence after watching this viral propaganda piece.

Chief of Staff Tony Rizzuto stood up and croaked, "Well, now we know where we stand."

"More like, knocked out cold on the canvas," someone muttered.

"In a word, yes. But there's more."

"More?!" The president's face was ashen. "Do not tell me any children died at that… school."

"Not at all. Kyle, would you?" Tony motioned to the computer tech. As the next clip began, he added, "This is security footage retrieved from the property. Here you see the man who earlier removed his mask, and is now exiting the church with his son and daughter—"

"Do we know that to be true?" Eileen asked.

"Yes. And here's how. Although the light was low, the camera was able to get definitive scans of both his eyes and face. The man's name is Morgan Haggerston. Does that ring a bell with anyone?"

The staff looked around at one another.

"I guess not," Eileen said. "Should it?"

"He was among the dozen or so inmates that escaped from the debtors' prison in Pennsylvania last summer."

"Wait a second," analyst Danielle Flanagan said. "That was a Sentinels' inside job coordinated with some of the guards, right?"

"Correct," Tony said. "The staff involved were disciplined severely. But of the fugitives, only two were caught in the ensuing months. So right now you may be thinking, 'Oh well, this Morgan fellow just went out looking for his kids.' "

"Who were what?" Eileen said testily. "Not put into the custody of other relatives? Not attending their normal schools, but instead sent off to… the wilderness? Because last I checked, I was still the president—but I really seem to be missing something here."

"This is all true," Tony said, maintaining his poise. "And your consternation is duly noted. But bear with me, because this all gets even more interesting."

"We are all most definitely interested. Proceed."

Eileen waved a hand, shaking her head in disbelief.

"Who else escaped with Morgan? James Haggerston, his father, who just so happened to come up in a recent face scan. How? Because the FBI was hauling in an agent of their own—who had gone AWOL while secretly embedded at the Mall of Absolution!"

"Hold on," Danielle said, raising a finger. "I heard about that through one of my… Well, never mind who. The point is, that action took place on a farm in Iowa, not Minnesota. How—and why—did an old man working for the Sentinels in Pennsylvania go all the way out there? And he went undetected the whole time?"

"It gets stranger." Rizzuto consulted a tablet. "This property where… Special Agent Marcus Young was apprehended, it too is owned by the Church of Modestianity. However, it actually functions as a medical facility for military veterans."

Eileen snapped out of the daze she had fallen into. "What?!"

"It's true. All high-level care. Nothing subversive or religious going on out there. We believe that is why James—a disabled Iraq War One veteran—was not also taken into custody."

Everyone in the meeting room started throwing out theories. After a few minutes, the president raised her hand for silence.

"So you're telling me," she said, "we've got an FBI agent who went rogue, possibly linking up with the father of the man we just saw at that children's camp? Who do I even go after here? This Morgan Haggerston or our own people? Jesus Christ, this is like Abu Ghraib all over again."

"Well," strategist Natalie Greer said, "according to

what I just pulled up, the whole Haggerston family was caught burning documents. So maybe the children…"

"Let's get real," the president retorted. "A lot of people are doing that—of all colors and stripes, too! No, no…" Eileen Jeffries-Lao's face tightened as she declared, "We're staring into the abyss now!"

Tony said, "There's no need to get maudlin here, Madam President. You won the election. You have the mandate. These are potholes, not bridge collapses."

"Still, an ugly bruise. Kids always pull the heartstrings, and we're on the wrong side of this one."

Natalie said, "Eileen, we know the optics look bad right now. But these programs all exist for a good reason. White anger is…" She trailed off as she watched Eileen bite into a pen. A moment later she quietly added, "From my understanding, the goal is to reroute the nerve from defiance to cooperation."

"I don't think we were in the wrong to fund an… insurance policy that took the form of these schools," Danielle said. "Look at it in the context of recent history. The colonial era had been over for decades, and Europe seemed poised to show the world what a multi-ethnic bloc could achieve. But then—" She compressed her lips.

"They rolled back the clock," Eileen said. "All the usual suspects, too."

"And a lot of their Italian, German, and British cousins are here in America."

"You know," Eileen said, leaning back into the padding of her chair, "has anyone really looked into the role that the migrant expulsions played in getting *us* elected in 'twenty-four? In stark contrast to the Europeans, we had a *plan* to right the ship *and* keep moving forward."

Danielle asked, "So you're saying it was more than

just disgust at what those other countries did?"

"Absolutely. The EU had this abstract idea that plopping millions of warm bodies into Europe would magically solve their debt and population problems. And who knows, maybe it could have worked. But people are not all plug-and-play with the exact same programming. Were their policy wonks simply too afraid to acknowledge even basic cultural differences for fear of being called racist? Is that really what prevented them from successfully integrating their new citizens?"

"We're the melting pot, not them," Kyle the tech guy chirped.

"Hmm," Jeffries-Lao said. "Their bureaucratic class has just always been so out of touch. Everything seems to take them by surprise! 'What, the migrants are congregating in ghettos?' 'What, the host population doesn't like being raped and stabbed?' I swear, so much of that terrible violence we saw earlier this decade was completely avoidable. And I—off the record, of course —put blame at the feet of complacent EU leaders. One, for not designing a plan that involved actual humans. And two, they forgot the capacity for barbarism among their own people."

Tony Rizzuto cleared his throat loudly. "This is great philosophy," he said, "but we'd better get back to the present. Because despite all *our* planning and recent win at the ballot box—critical eyes are looking our way. How many millions of Americans are now thinking about those sad children in South Carolina?"

Eileen leaned forward, rubbing her hands as she said, "This is all so complex. To navigate history. To try and bring out the best in all people. To inspire. To assist. Especially now when people flinch if a new idea doesn't arrive wrapped in foam. I mean, you can't just say, 'Hey, let's give all the Caucs partial lobotomies,' am I right?"

Everyone laughed nervously. Tony said, "I wouldn't be in favor of that, actually. Because I've got perfect hair."

"No, no," the president cackled. "I'm just riffing on the political magic arts. To get not just yourself, but entire populations from here to there... You've got to balance subtle moves with the public policies that are there for all to see. I'm afraid we've missed the mark on that first part, and now we're paying the price with this terrible PR."

Eileen Jeffries-Lao stood up and shook her fist

"I *never* liked the idea of debtors' prisons," she said, "but they talked me into it. Said *enforcement* was the key to collections. Those GI Joe types were probably just salivating about all the new military toys our budget could pay for. You want to lock up the adults? Fine, fine. Set an example to other would-be document deniers. But abducting their children! I hate to say this, but it's times like these when we really need to ask ourselves if we've lost our way. Who knows, maybe it would have been better for Dominguez to win, and then everybody could have watched him stumble around knocking over everything we built."

Danielle tilted a notepad downward and started writing as she said, "So how do you want to respond to the crisis at hand? I worry that condemnation, even while also pleading no foreknowledge, could still come back to bite us. Perhaps stressing *reform* under the larger HRA-wide rehabilitation project will help cover our bases."

"Some heads will have to roll, though." Eileen sat down again. "Gonna need to have at least a couple fall guys on this one. *Real* this time, too."

"Understood." Danielle gave a devilish grin. "Let's go with the Colonel Kurtz narrative. Some career civil servant—left to his own devices, with too much funding but not enough oversight—he just took it too far."

"Jesus," the president said, running a hand through her hair. "Even when we spin, the big picture makes us look like we don't know what we're doing. My god, spending the next four years fending off scandals is no way to run a presidency, let alone a program like the HRA."

"It's happened before," Kyle said. "Iran-Contra pretty much tied Reagan's hands. But still, the Berlin Wall came down not long after he rode off into the sunset."

Eileen sighed. She said, "The fact is, moving money to where it needs to go isn't enough to sustain us anymore. The deeper the HRA gets entrenched, the more complicated it all becomes. Dents on the hull, tangled nets, and then of course there's the crew…"

"Don't lose hope," Tony said. "It's only a few drunken sailors, not a full-on mutiny."

"Ha! Half the country is itching for a revolt. Anyway, I think we're done here. Time for *us* to get a little drunk. Because there's some choppy seas between now and January of 2033."

"Aye, aye, skipper."

16. SURROUNDED BY FOOLS

"What's up, Mister Flop?" Nolan set down his fork and chomped on a pickle spear.

"Oh, you know," Clyde said, dropping his bag into the booth opposite Nolan as he sat down. "Just thinking about the next solo track, I guess."

"That's a good attitude," Nolan said, mopping up ketchup with a steak fry. "Learn anything from song number two?"

Clyde's eyes wandered across the diner. It was nicer than most other places nearby. He said, "How quick people forget, even *after* you hit big. This one got played for like two days, then nothing."

"Okay, so you're paying attention. That's good. The fact that you actually followed up with something is a plus. But you know, the song probably just wasn't all that great. Video looked pretty good—even if I would have done a few things differently."

"Oh yeah? Funny, I heard you were booked the day we made it." Clyde reached over and grabbed a french fry.

"C'mon now, DJC," Nolan said, falling away with a smile. "Don't hurt me! Nah, of course that's right. I had some stuff going on out of town."

"New stuff or… old stuff?"

"Who want to know?" Nolan stared at Clyde, who matched his gaze. "S'alright, kid. I'm just probing you. See who you are now that the spotlight's faded a bit."

"I'm the same old Clyde, I think. But what about you? Little while since the Pigeon Man was laid to rest or whatever. How's the new Nolan doin'?"

"Well," Nolan said, gathering his papers and tucking a few dollar bills under the check, "let me show you what I've got cooking. Walk with me back to the crib."

Nolan handed the receipt tray to the hostess on their way out and said, "Nice to see you again."

"Any change?" the woman asked.

"Never. You keep it, treat y'all selves to something nice."

The woman smiled. "Have a wonderful day, Mr. Simmons."

They stepped outside and Clyde started gyrating his body wildly. He said in a falsetto voice, "Ooh, Mr. Simmons!"

"Yeah, well," Nolan said with a wave of the hand, "you only mock because you don't yet understand the value of how everyday people can make your life a little more pleasant."

"I think you just like flirting with them waitresses."

"That's 'cause you still got your mama cooking you nice meals. I got operations to run, no time to cook. Fast food and delivery are one thing, but sometimes it's nice to get that human connection. Be treated right."

Clyde kicked at a small branch that had fallen onto the sidewalk. "But then you got to pay extra. The tip."

"And it's worth it too. For good service. A waitress that's on point will make you feel good for the rest of the day."

"How's that?" Clyde asked. "She smile at you? Shake her booty?"

"Sometimes, yeah." Nolan grinned. "But you seat me with a old lady who got her timing down right? That's gold right there. Refill your coffee when it need it, give you time to eat your soup before bringing out your sandwich... and no unnecessary interruptions all the while. I swear, it's a real treat. In fact, I wish I was still hungry just so I could go back and do it again!"

"You crazy, Nolan." Clyde stuffed his hands into his hoodie pockets and shook his head.

They came to a stop at the corner of an intersection. As they waited for the signal to change, a car going in their direction pulled up behind another idling car. The driver side door opened slightly and a pile of trash dumped out onto the pavement. The light turned green and a second later the car was moving forward in traffic.

"Did you see that?" Nolan said bitterly.

"What happened?" Clyde looked all around the intersection.

"That mofo in the Mercedes just threw a bunch of garbage out from his car."

"Yeah?"

"Look at it." Nolan pointed. "Paper bag. Wrapper. Fries box. And a cup. Dude had some drive-thru, scarfed it down, and that was that. God damn! Can't believe people be doin' that in their own hoods."

"Maybe he don't live around here." Clyde stepped into the crosswalk.

"Whatever. Anyway, Clyde. Keep doing what you need to do for you. Don't waste your time worrying about these types of people no more. You've already given enough. And them?" Nolan waved a hand behind him. "Every day—in the little things like that right there—they prove they ain't worth none of it."

"He probably wanted to keep his car clean." Clyde bobbed his head up and down. "Mercedes are tight!"

"Are you serious? What about the neighborhood itself? Why not just squat down and take a shit in the street?"

"Nolan, you too much, man. It's just a little trash, it'll blow away."

Nolan gave Clyde's shoulder a squeeze. He said, "I'll forgive you because you're just a kid. But Clyde, it's the small, everyday things that define you, reveal who you are. See, that dude probably wears diamond earrings, keeps his car spotless. But in that one moment right there, he showed us who he really is on the inside."

"Damn," Clyde remarked, "you got all that from one thing?"

"Yes, sir. It says, 'I'm lazy. I don't care about anyone else. I'm only living in the moment.' That's how he lets us know he doesn't want to be a part of this community."

"Why you so mad at that man? You maybe know him from somewhere else?"

"No, I don't know him! It's because he just took a mini-shit on every one of his neighbors, that's why."

"Haha, maybe he call himself MC Mini-Shit!" Clyde began to riff, "Yo, I be a hungry rapper. Fill the street with my beats, and chicken sandwich wrappers. Mad respect or I'll… use the gutter as a crapper! Step off, y'all!"

Nolan couldn't help but smile. "This is why we got to get you out of here. Talent like that, you should be a million miles away from this mess."

Clyde nudged Nolan's arm. "You still here. And you smarter than me."

"Boy," Nolan sighed, "I've been trying to help. Really thought I could. Kept a lot of you youngins out of the nets, but… It just burns you out seeing so many get eaten up."

"Don't quit, I'm serious. Without you, nothing ever would have happened for me. I know it."

Nolan stopped, turned to Clyde. "Thank you, young man. Guess I'm at a turning point. Met a really nice lady at one of those speeches. Lives down in Connecticut. So we been talkin'…"

"Wait… Is she white?"

Nolan looked over at Clyde and gave a sly smile. "Yep. But she got a real figure on her, boy!"

"Aw, man!" Clyde began to shadow box down the sidewalk. "Nolan… be rollin'… Gave a lil' talk… fell in love with a Cauc!"

"Clyde, Clyde, Clyde. You are some kind of mad genius. But if I do it—really get out of here—will you promise to follow my lead?"

"I don't know, man. Before all this blew up, I just wanted to say something for my people. Can't expect everything to just get better overnight."

"That's noble. But listen to me. Sometimes you can do the most good by stepping away. I think your music might be able to help people from all over. But you can't do it when you're surrounded by fools who, one way or another, are going to drag you down."

"Well, maybe *you* can just up and go. I got my family here. Tee especially, he needs me."

"I understand," Nolan said. "Just remember, I'm not blowing smoke up your you-know-what when I say you're an exceptional talent. I don't want to get all sentimental, but it's a tragedy for the world when God's gifts don't reach their potential. And I've seen it happen before."

Clyde bowed his head, saying, "That's too much, Nolan. Don't give me all that. I mean, should I sign on with Pryor and move out to Cali, or what?"

"Possibly. Just really think about how much more you'd probably achieve in a place where there ain't trash sitting all over the place."

Clyde looked at a crumpled can that had been jammed into a nearby bush. "They don't want to fly," he said quietly. "They'll get down with my song and dance to it… but they won't take my hand and come up to the roof to see. Damn…"

Nolan threw his arm around Clyde and gave him a fatherly squeeze. "Don't feel too sad, bro. I know this dump can get to you. But there's good people out there. Fighting the battle in every city. They don't have your way with words, but they'll understand your message. So write for them, inspire them not to give up. You just don't have to do it from the inside of a toilet bowl to keep your street cred."

"C'mon, you know that ain't me." Clyde then muttered, "I don't have any street cred."

"That's right, 'cause you're a good kid. We got to change your location—improve your situation—to help save the nation. Such is the equation!"

"Haha," Clyde said, pulling away. "That's a good rap, Nolan."

"All part of today's lesson," Simmons said with a grin. "But now, that's a wrap! Come on into the studio, check out some of the improvements we got goin' on."

17. PARALYZED

Chris Donohugh kept thinking about his friend Glenn's email on the subway ride home.

"Hey, Shredder!" the message had read. "I played those new riffs you wrote for the other guys. They were impressed! And now that you've upgraded your rig, they definitely want to hear more."

Glenn was of course writing in code. Because for all of his own band nostalgia on that solitary night when Kate was out of town last week, Chris had not once touched a guitar.

But he had made use of the software that copied the work emails on Kate's home laptop and sent them to his own computer two rooms away. To keep his conscience from a complete meltdown, he had as an extra precautionary measure coded a crawler to meticulously erase all personally identifying information contained within these messages.

His final step in thwarting the HRA's increased IT security was to purchase a used laptop with cash from a pawn shop. After several hard drive wipes and software modifications, he used it to send Glenn the encrypted data from public locations like cafes and bars.

And no one in the world could ever possibly guess the file's password: VotingBoothSarcophagus. This being the title of the last song Raucous Voice ever wrote, but never played live or recorded before the group disbanded nearly a decade ago. The phrase had been an ongoing inside joke between Chris and Glenn ever since.

Chris knew from a quick manual scan of Kate's messages that there was nothing particularly juicy in these first batches. But there was no telling how many other hacked HRA email accounts were also being fed into the underground's growing database, where perhaps bits of her conversations would make sense within the larger context.

"The people's MARVIN," Chris said ruefully as he trotted up his building's front steps. A smile fought its way to the surface against the pressure of his clenched jaws.

Once inside his apartment, he felt his stomach churn while thinking about the last line of Glenn's encoded message. The "upgrade" referred to was Kate's promotion to liaison between the HRA and the White House. Despite the felonies he'd already committed, somehow only now did the Jeffries-Lao connection bring the phrase "threat to national security" to mind.

Chris wasn't sure he could keep doing this. He might have been able to sleep soundly next to Kate, even while the bits of confidential data were flying through the walls from her computer to his, if it was just regular HRA office stuff. But now, when it appeared that she would be spending many nights in another bed two hundred miles away, he was mortified that someone on the White House staff might catch wind of his activities.

Next would come the wrath of the president's digital espionage team. A soap-opera scandal that all the networks would dig their teeth into. The haunted look of betrayal on Kate's face through the plexiglass divider in the jail's visiting room—assuming she even came to see him. And himself in an orange jumpsuit, just like his high school band had worn as gag costumes at live shows.

Chris was starting to feel nauseous now. He paced around the apartment several times as the gravity of what he had already done began to sink in. If there was no way back—no magical undo command like computers had—there was also no way out or forward. He would probably have to sink down into the mud and hide with this lie for the rest of his life.

Because he couldn't afford to lose Kate. He'd already gone through those hypothetical emotions months ago during her cancer scare, and watched his hair nearly turn gray in the process.

On the other hand, he was at least certain that Glenn wouldn't rat him out if he was ever arrested for conspiring with the Sentinels. The bonds that musicians formed in a tour van were stronger than anything known to man, except perhaps actual combat soldiers.

And it was a two-way street, apparently. How else to explain Chris agreeing to spy on his wife during that drunken reunion with Glenn several weeks ago?

Chris opened the file cabinet drawer in his office and fished out the little device he'd used to pair the two computers. The urge to crush it was followed by the desperate desire to plug it back into Kate's laptop and uninstall the spyware. To at least hide his tracks, if he couldn't erase the deed and its consequences.

But he was paralyzed. He wouldn't do anything

right now. Not for Kate. Not for Glenn. Not to protect the president. And definitely not to help the Sentinels.

Chris didn't even know what he could do to save himself.

He saw the top of a softshell guitar case poking out of the open closet door. Instinctively he glanced at the shrine to Raucous Voice on his bookshelf. A crushing sadness came over him in the silence of the room.

I should've written a new song after all.

18. HISTORICAL LANDMARK

Eileen Jeffries-Lao never expected something like this to happen to her. If asked months ago, before it had started, she would have honestly answered that she didn't even *want* it.

But in the weeks leading up to the election—suddenly stressful and chaotic and her campaign *vulnerable*—she had just spent so much time with her chief of staff Tony Rizzuto, that she found herself falling into his arms late one night in October.

Weeks later and she was still trying to make sense of having this side of herself awakened. Her marriage had been on ice for years, in the carnal sense. First Man Paul Jeffries was of course known for his wandering eye—and more—during most of their public lives, but Eileen had been able rationalize it away because *she* was the rising political star. Later still, as she was leading the Reparations movement that was righting so many wrongs, his infidelity seemed a small personal price to pay.

Whether it was the unexpected late-hour election

threat from Victor Dominguez, or understanding that even in victory her political career would be over within a few years, Eileen Jeffries-Lao had stumbled into an affair with one of her male subordinates and now clung onto it greedily.

Besides, Tony had been her rock for years. Now Eileen was just... leaning in a little more.

Tonight would be their last evening together before Tribesgiving. Tony was flying to Arkansas with his family tomorrow, so now she kissed him with extra intensity. It had been so long since a man had made her feel such passion.

"Tony," she cooed. "You have no idea where that last... dance took me."

The man gave her shoulder a squeeze. "Maybe not. But I know when what I'm doing is working."

"Mm-hmm... I'll miss you when you're away. Will Alana give you what you need?"

"Let's not talk about that," Tony said. "All we gotta do is get through the holidays, New Year's, your inauguration... then the world is ours."

"God, I adore you," she said. "You see the road ahead so clearly. If people really knew how much of their president is just me acting out what you and the others have prepared... they'd call me a fraud."

Tony reached his free hand onto the bedside table and picked up the TV remote.

He said, "Hey now, Miss Lao. Why don't we watch something, take your mind off all that for awhile?"

"Sure, sure. I've been a bad girl today. Asked for alone time before Wall Street even closed. You better put on some news first, check the headlines."

Tony Rizzuto pulled up one of the twenty-four-hour news channels. Immediately he perked up. A graphic on screen indicated there was breaking news. He felt

Eileen adjust onto an elbow beside him.

"...truly stunning announcement," the reporter was saying. "Today a lawsuit was filed in the state of California by a group of young Beneficiaries seeking to contest the compulsory aspects of Direct Descendant Match..."

"What?!" Eileen blurted. She was up on her knees in a flash, then turned her face back toward Tony with questioning eyes. He just nodded back in the direction of the screen.

"Let's listen," he said.

"...formally submitted by attorney Sabine L. Plotz, a rising legal star who is no stranger to HRA-related disputes."

The next shot showed Ms. Plotz standing outside a courthouse while flanked by a dozen Minoricans. She said, "Today I stand with these brave youngsters to help guide their mission toward success. They are here to say, 'We may be Beneficiaries, but we've already had enough of this Reparations millstone!' I hope to do them justice every step of the way."

"Oh, turn it off!" Eileen gasped. She fell back onto a pillow.

"You want to talk about this?" Tony said.

"Absolutely not," she said, staring up at the ceiling. "Not tonight. Please, just change the channel."

"Okay, no problem."

Tony began flipping through the TV stations. Eileen wiggled around and rested her head on his leg. He could hear her mutter, "No... no... no..." as he surfed. Finally he felt her playfully whack his shin.

"Yeah!" she said. "Let's watch this."

One glimpse of the man wearing khaki shorts and retro safari hat, and Tony knew exactly what he was in for.

"Alright," he chuckled. "I didn't realize you were such a fan. Good old Rog…"

"Turn it up," she said, nestling down into his thigh.

Tony did as she asked, then eased back onto the headboard to watch.

On screen the world-famous Australian TV host Roger Stephens was walking through a brightly lit office-laboratory. The camera trailed behind as he spoke with animated gestures.

"…what fascinates me the most about what we do is something I call Pre-Singularity Studies." Stephens held up a pink external hard drive, saying, "A period of somebody's whole life is stored inside here. Pictures, emails, hopes, dreams… An entire time capsule stockpiled in this one little plastic case. And it's dated… 2015. Hmm… Right before politics hit that crucial tipping point, and then wrenched us all into the monocultural divide which we're still grappling with today."

The host set down the hard drive, then looked at the camera intently.

"Oh yes," he said, "and *that* is why I do what I do. Rather than chase wild animals or search for sunken ships full of coins—I seek *humanity*. Our loves, our passions, our history. For I am… Rog the Hard Drive Hunter! Join me tonight on this ultimate adventure, as my team pursues a lead that could change the course of life as we know it… forever!"

After the show's opening credit sequence, Roger reappeared in the back of an equipment van that was bounding down a rough road in near-darkness.

"Our journey takes us to rural West Texas," his recorded voice said. "It was here that for decades industry prepared recyclable items before they were shipped to China for final processing. However, extreme fluctuations in the market price of raw materials often meant that these types of businesses would shut down without warning. Which is why we've traveled all the way out to the modern-day ghost town of Clint, Texas."

The van pulled up to a tall security barrier. Rog stepped out of the side door and pointed into the distance beyond. He said, "Our team was alerted by an anonymous source about the massive warehouse you see past this reinforced perimeter. And it just might contain… the mother lode! Shall we?"

In the hazy blue and orange pre-dawn light, Rog and three other team members slipped through a freshly cut breach in the fencing. The camera crew kept pace as they approached.

The team gathered outside a fortified iron door. Rog said, "We've just wired the frame with cutter charges. This should disable the locking mechanism without doing any further damage—or worse yet, starting a fire. Are we ready now?"

Everyone ran behind a rusted-out dumpster. A series of jarring cracks could be heard. The camera pointed back toward the door and revealed a great deal of smoke and dust rising into the air.

"We're in!" Rog waved an arm. They sprinted to the door, threw it open, and turned flashlights on as they ran inside the cavernous warehouse. The team scattered and moved cautiously through a network of dark and dusty aisles.

The next shot showed Roger leaning forward with his hands pressed against a giant metal object whose sides angled inward from the top, as if it were an inverted pyramid. He was shaking his head from side to side while staring at the ground.

Finally he turned to the camera and joined his hands

as if in prayer. "Ladies and gentlemen, this is indeed the moment we've all be working toward. Years of our lives dedicated in faithful pursuit. Now, I present to you... the Treasure of the Terabyte Madre!"

He took a camera into his hand and scaled the monolith's attached ladder fifteen feet up to the lip. It was uncovered and filled nearly to the top with... something. Rog swung the camera around and its spotlight revealed hundreds of small plastic rectangles of different shapes and colors.

He began to laugh maniacally. Suddenly the camera lurched down five feet—he had jumped into the container!

A hand was seen poring through the objects, scooping them up and then casting them aside like playing cards. A loud crunch came from behind and then the camera was passed off. Roger backed away and fell to his knees.

Visibly shaking and nearly babbling through tears, he said, "This is... it. The Holy Grail that we at *Hard Drive Hunters* always dreamed of. Because this is not simply the recent history of a nation. No, it's also perhaps a priceless tool that will aid MARVIN in his quest to compile the ultimate, most comprehensive record of humankind ever. Oh yes, ladies and gentlemen, they really did back everything up... right here!"

Rog started humming a tune and took a yellow case into his hand. He bounced it on his palm as if gauging the weight, then flipped it over to inspect the information label. He took a small device from his breast pocket and scanned the bar code.

"Oh my goodness!" Rog gave a thumbs-up. "This drive dates all the way back to 2006. Now, it's not a very large capacity storage device by modern standards.

But perhaps it contains recordings of an old man born in the early part of the twentieth century recounting his life. Or maybe scans of legal documents tracing a family's property holdings going back two hundred years. It could be anything…"

He fell forward and began to swim playfully across the lake of hard drives. "Do you understand what I'm saying?" he wailed. "Ten thousand of them in just this one vat alone. Maybe a *million* drives in the whole facility." He sat up, smiling gaily. "And to think that for years law enforcement has been chasing down individual Debtors for vandalizing a few documents— meanwhile this incomprehensible trove of data has been sitting here unguarded the entire time. Just imagine how many person-hours this restoration project will take. Hint, hint. We'll be hiring!"

Rog exhaled profoundly, then said in a somber voice, "By the authority vested in me by our generous sponsors at the Historical Reparations Administration, I, Roger Stephens, hereby declare this property, the former Leary Metals, Inc., to be a landmark of historical significance. It shall be afforded all the legal protections therein."

As the end credits rolled, an announcer said, "Join us next time on *Hard Drive Hunters*, as we journey once more into civilization's forgotten corners in search of digital gold…"

Tony Rizzuto glanced away from the television and saw that his mistress, the President of the United States, was fast asleep.

19. PRIVATE AUDIENCE

"Your Prescience, it's an honor to finally meet you."

Matthias Witherspoon was seated comfortably across from the Prescient One in an antique-style chair which had Modestian imagery carved into the wood, as well as within the upholstery. A servant had just delivered tea before closing the doors on the church leader's private study.

"Likewise, Reverend."

As Matthias casually glanced around, he was surprised that the room seemed so... conventional. He had heard rumors from various church members that this man was a quirky interior decorator.

"Looking for something?" the man in electric blue attire asked him.

"Oh, just soaking in the mood," Witherspoon said. "Seems very relaxing, but also conducive to getting work done. I have a small office tucked away at my church where I compose many of my Sunday sermons."

"Indeed?" The Prescient One smiled. "I recently had these quarters remodeled. Everything seems to have become much more serious lately. I couldn't focus with all that blue rope dangling from the ceiling."

Matthias was unable to suppress a grin.

"Oh?" the church leader said almost playfully. "So you knew about the old look in here? Well, if that's the worst bit of gossip people are spreading…"

"I assure you I've heard nothing else."

"Now, Matthias," the Prescient One said, "please do accept my apologies for not being available sooner. As Modestianity grows, there are always a million little things that require my personal attention. Blessings, lectures—but surely you know all that from your own church duties."

"Ha, yes. And no matter how much you've delegated, someone always needs something."

"Surely. But tell me, now that you've lived intimately among us for nearly two weeks, what are your thoughts on our upstart new religion?"

Witherspoon took a sip of tea. He said, "To be honest with you, I was in a daze for the first little while. Felt like a fish out of water, second-guessing my decision to leave my people behind during this sabbatical. And then, seeing everyone so happy here, singing songs, getting work done—every day I was just *waiting* for someone to hand me some sort of cryptic note."

"Oh, really? Saying what?"

"Maybe a plea for help or warning me to leave. I don't know…"

The Prescient One shook his head and smiled. "That's all so twentieth century. I suppose there's been some real *cults* in the Internet Age, but nothing on the scale of Modestianity. Could you imagine if we really had, what, sex dungeons in the basements? With all the tiny cameras and sensors everywhere? We'd be exposed in a heartbeat!"

"That's not really my area of expertise. But maybe someone was blackmailing you. Or…" Matthias paused. "Well, that was part of what I came here to find out. If you were for real."

"Aha, so this *wasn't* purely a spiritual quest for you, Mr. Witherspoon. Interesting. You came also to snoop around. Why? Or more to the point, for whom?"

"For myself, dammit!" Matthias nearly yelled. "Before I went and made any other big life changes, I had to be sure you were legit. The real deal. I couldn't be no sucka—a fool!—like I'd been makin' these men act all up in those prisons!"

Reverend Witherspoon sat back in a huff. The Prescient One stood up, then reached into a desk drawer and pulled out a small picture frame. He handed it to Matthias before returning to his seat.

"Look at that face," the Prescient One said. "That was me fifteen years ago. When I was just a regular fellow working in the video gaming world. We all change, Matthias. Sometimes for the better, sometimes not. But as *you* must surely preach, no man or woman is permitted to give up on his chance at redemption."

Matthias wiped an eye with the back of his hand. "No, we're not."

"I don't blame you for projecting your own regrets onto my church. That suspicion not only brought you here, but led you to a much closer examination of who we are. Trust me, I'm well aware that many of our members first came here out of material desperation, and not faith. But what good is a religion if it is solely focused on the ethereal and doesn't aid people in their daily lives?"

"Hale-Bopp," Matthias said and chuckled to himself. "To the stars and beyond."

The Prescient One nodded solemnly.

"So the question is, Reverend Witherspoon, what will you decide to do now that you've confirmed in your heart that we are pure? We would be honored if you converted to Modestianity. And I would personally attend the ceremony."

Matthias handed the frame back. He looked down into his hands and said, "I could. And maybe I should. I have so much to learn. But that would be the easy way. Or… the popular choice. Because to do that would say to my people, 'Hey y'all, these guys over here seem more effective, so let's run into their corner while the gettin's good.' "

The Prescient One smiled warmly. "And we would welcome them all."

"But we already have our God. We have our Holy Scriptures."

"The spiritual—"

"But no!" Witherspoon said, shaking his fist. "These folks have their homes, their families… their *way of life*. Who am I to tell them to drop everything and follow some white man—or blue man, whatever the hell color you paint yourself—why should they follow you, when there's no commonality at the *root?*"

"Perhaps," the sage said after a pause. "But Modestianity is the ultimate colorblind religion because it's so new. We have no dusty old baggage. No mistranslated texts. No feuds, no prejudices…"

Matthias laughed, almost angrily. He said, "Then it's even more irrelevant to my people. *We do* have baggage. We got real history!"

The Prescient One brought his hands together. "So your choice is this. Just let it all go here with us and make a fresh start. Or do you have the courage to dig in and tear everything apart?"

"We have no choice, Your Prescience. I *got* to find the strength to face what's inside. Hold up every beautiful silk shirt and every stained pair of drawers we got packed in that suitcase we been carrying around. It's the only way forward."

The Prescient One folded his arms over the picture frame and nodded definitively. "So you've come to a decision," he said. "I'm glad, truly."

Matthias laid his palms on his knees and rocked his head from side to side. His eyes were closed. Slowly a smile transformed his tense face. He looked up at the Prescient One. "Now I see. You *are* a wise man. A good man."

"I thank you, Matthias. It is my belief that you are one as well."

Witherspoon clapped his hands together. He said happily, "I shall call you the King of Clarity. Or maybe... the Dean of Dialectic."

"You honor me," the Prescient One said, smiling once more. "While most people do know in their hearts what they want, sometimes they have to put it into words to see what's required to achieve it."

"Mmm... So you couldn't just *send* me home. Because *telling* me that this was the right thing to do would leave my mind full of doubt every step of the way back to my church. But as soon as *I* said those words..."

The reverend's face eased into an expression of total satisfaction.

"We make a pretty good team, don't we?" the Prescient One said. "When the dust settles on all this political chaos, perhaps one day you and I will have the opportunity to share a unified message with the American people."

"I would like that. Very much." Matthias cleared

his throat. "But I've got a lot of work to do between now and then. If this whole Reparations thing is about to go away, I need to prepare my people."

"Indeed. But don't feel as if you have to fight the battles alone, Reverend. Call on us for any insights or assistance you might need."

Matthias rose and took the Prescient One's right hand into his own hands. "Sir, I don't know how to thank you for all that your existence has done to put me back on the straight and narrow. Truly, I had lost my way." He shook his head to try and stifle a chuckle, then continued, "I know the Lord doesn't always give us the road map, but damn if I still can't believe that it was your kooky Modestian family that—"

A booming flash came out of nowhere. Matthias felt himself stumble across the room. He landed painfully on his left side. Rolling back onto his elbows, he saw the space filling with smoke in the half-light. Suddenly a number of black-clad figures fanned out with weapons drawn.

Matthias, stunned into near-deafness, cowered in the shadows as he watched the bright cape of the Prescient One hoisted up into the air. He lay in stupefied horror as the stormtroopers carried the Modestian leader out of the room through the breach.

A light flashed into his eyes. He raised a sore arm in front of his face, but an instant later the light moved away. He found himself alone in the Prescient One's bombed-out private chambers.

After several tense minutes, Matthias cautiously made his way out of the smoky room. He wandered blindly down a dark corridor, and as his hearing slowly returned, tragic wails echoed through the Church of Modestianity's inner sanctum.

The Prescient One was gone.

20. RIDING THE WIND

Arizona Senator Victor Dominguez was back home in Flagstaff for the Tribesgiving recess. He'd enjoyed simple pleasures like driving his three children to school, even if Michael the oldest made a stink about not being able to ride on the bus with his friends.

The home-cooked meals around the family table with Jaclyn at his side almost enabled Victor to dial back the clock and forget the whirlwind that he had just lived for the past year. He tried to savor these quiet moments at home, rather than replay for the thousandth time all that could have been.

He knew that people faced defeat every day. His daughter's youth basketball team had lost just the other evening, in fact. Victor's election failure happened to be on a national stage and with much bigger stakes, however. But as he had told little Yasmin, she would have to learn from the loss and put it behind her—because there were many more games left for her to play in life. Many shots to take, and other important challenges to stand up to.

The senator tried to internalize all this while driving home alone after having dropped off his youngest child Nina at a morning playdate. But he suspected that his own defeat more resembled that of a young sports phenom who entered the professional leagues too early, and then for various reasons never peaked during his career. Would the Rebellican Party really nominate him again in four years? What headspace would the country even be in at that time?

No, on paper he seemed destined to serve perhaps two or three terms in the Senate, before moving on to lucrative work as a consultant or lobbyist. Had he really consigned himself to all that when delivering his concession speech on Election Night?

At the last second Victor veered his truck onto I-17 South instead of continuing directly home. Because that new option on his life's horizon had the power to throw his name right back in the ring—and he needed to consult with a trusted friend before making that crucial decision.

After an hour's drive down to Cottonwood, Victor stepped out of the vehicle and quietly approached the long curved wall of stone. He placed a small bundle of flowers into the mounted vase, then closed his eyes for a moment.

"Hello, Papa," he said. "I'm sorry for not coming to see you much lately. But I hope you can understand."

Victor rested a hand on the marble plaque that honored the late Eugenio Dominguez.

"And now I must ask for your advice. You see, I've been on such a wild journey these past few years— always rising, rising—and just when it seemed to have ended, and I was starting to make peace with that... Suddenly a new path opened up again. And frankly, Father, it has me terrified."

Senator Dominguez gazed down the length of the memorial wall. So many lives sealed behind the marble and stone. Dead, but not forgotten, he hoped.

Victor found that he was uncomfortable speaking like this, as if all the ghosts here might listen in on his private thoughts. He stepped away from his father's grave and began to stroll around the Catholic cemetery's contoured grounds.

"Oh Papa... I have always wanted to make you proud. You risked so much when you came to this country, but everything was simpler in your time. Wake up early, go to work, unclog people's drains, come home with the paycheck for Mama to buy us dinner. But now, for me..."

Victor trailed off. His attention had been caught by some sort of large bird that was arcing and swinging across the sky, and barely needing to flap its wings as it deftly rode the wind. He resumed his walk, all the while keeping this bird visible out of the corner of his eye.

"This opportunity... I keep asking myself, will it be good for the country? Because I already know what it could do for *me*. So Papa, now I must know, is this what *you* would have wanted me to do? Because although you never fully lost your accent, I know how important it was to you and Mama that Rita and I were *American*.

"But the 1970 or even 2000 version of that word is quite different from what it has meant lately. If your generation was forced to add the hyphen, it signified that you had chosen to *become* a Mexican-American. Today it seems to be the opposite. We aren't all Americans now—we're all just *in* America.

"And Father, I fear that this new... proposed venture is less about pride than it is about power.

Seizing it and flaunting it angrily. Your immigrant's humility is being replaced by… something very unpleasant, just because people can."

Victor started moving back toward his truck. He said, "Cornelius Alemán seems more interested in assembling an army than even a voting bloc. He wants me to help give his movement legitimacy. But—he says there are others, many others in business and politics who have already joined him. I could lose a great deal simply by refusing this man, if he still succeeds without me.

"Oh Papa, I miss hearing your wise words. But I'm afraid that your mind couldn't handle the choices we are required to make in today's world. Perhaps it is better that you have passed on."

Dominguez took a last look at the mausoleum wall through his windshield. The people of the past were filed away and suspended in that silent geometric grid. But *he* still had life flowing through him.

Victor vowed that he would not allow himself to be hushed, or manipulated, or forced into doing anything that went against what he knew to be right.

After a quiet prayer of thanks, he started the engine and began the drive home.

21. THE BRIGHTEST STAR

Clyde Jenkins didn't like what he heard coming from upstairs. His sister Myra and her boyfriend Octavius were arguing over something. Again.

He glanced over at his nephew Tyrell—Myra's first kid, but fathered by another guy who was out of the picture. The boy was intently focused on the video game they were playing, his fingers moving across the controller faster than Clyde could believe.

"You ain't playin'," Tyrell said.

"Sorry."

Clyde returned his focus to the enormous TV on which a dozen military personnel were stealthily moving toward the perimeter of a fort. Tracer bullets began to whiz past as the group neared the fence.

"Find cover!" Tyrell commanded.

"Where do I go?" Clyde said.

"Behind that truck… Run!"

One of the soldiers on screen fell in a burst of red spray, but all of the others safely made their way behind a burnt-out troop transport vehicle.

"Now what do we do?" Clyde asked. "We're still taking heat."

Tyrell looked down at his controller and pressed a dizzying combination of buttons. He said, "I got to order up some bombs."

"Oh yeah? One of these dudes here got like a bazooka in his bag?"

"Nah. Hold up. You'll see."

A moment later a dull roar came out of the surround-sound speakers, then the TV screen filled with orange flame and a billowing mushroom cloud.

"Yeah!" Tyrell said. "Let's move out..."

Clyde smiled. His little nephew already knew this war game well enough to call in the airstrikes. Then he heard a real-time thud come down through the living room ceiling. He wondered if *he* should call the police...

Probably not. He'd wait to see what his mother would do. She was in her bedroom upstairs and would know if... or when... to intervene.

"Aw... now you dead!" Tyrell said.

Clyde had let his soldier trail behind the group and an enemy rifleman who had survived the bombing shot him through the head.

"Sorry," Clyde said. "Get into that base without me, I guess."

"No doubt."

"Hey, I'ma take a break until you get to the next level."

Clyde went into the kitchen and opened the fridge to grab a soda. It was packed with leftovers from the previous day's feast. The Jenkins family, for all its imperfections, truly did have a lot to be grateful for this Tribesgiving.

He took his goose down jacket from a chairback

and stepped out onto the little patio that was behind the family's condo. He glanced up at the lighted window of the room that Myra and Octavius shared. Their daughter Sarah was probably inside with them too. Things seemed to have quieted down for the moment.

Clyde sipped his drink, easing back onto the wood railing as he looked at the sky. Pockets of stars revealed themselves as the clouds moved past. He focused on a particularly bright star and waited for it to reappear after each cloud.

He wondered which part of this scene he was supposed to be. The cloud in motion, making its way across the land—or the shimmering light sitting as a fixed guide?

A muffled shout came through the upstairs window. It was the same kind of lovers' quarrel he had been witness to since the succession of his mother's boyfriends during his own childhood. At least those guys barely laid a hand on him—he'd heard some pretty rough stories of abuse from other kids he knew growing up.

Clyde exhaled wearily. He'd tried his best to set everything up nice. With all that money his song "Fly So High" brought in, the least he could do was try to give Myra and her kids a better place to call home away from the old neighborhood. And he did like Octavius too—a hard-edged guy to be sure, but one who always came at Clyde straight.

Still, Clyde was only a teenager. After every fight that took place under the roof that his magic money had provided, he sensed that there were just some things he couldn't understand, or fix.

He thought about his recent talk with Nolan. The mentor who seemed adamant that Clyde "sell out to get out." Or was it more accurately, get out to survive? To leave these streets where people still fought and shit and screamed as if nothing good had ever come their way.

Clyde heard the patio door open. Tyrell poked his head out.

"I'ma go to bed in a minute," the boy said.

"Oh yeah?" Clyde smiled. "Lemme come in and say good night then."

A half hour later and all was quiet in the Jenkins residence. Clyde had helped his nephew get ready for sleep, and all the while he didn't hear any sounds from the other bedrooms. He didn't know if Octavius had slipped out for some Friday night action while he was standing on the patio, but usually it was best to leave others to their own business.

Clyde went back down to the living room and started flipping through the channels, although he wasn't really paying attention. He still felt uneasy, like he was butting up against some sort of invisible barrier. What was it?

Sometimes he just wanted to roll up to a club and let the remaining DJC mystique attract whatever good times might be had. But the people close to him kept saying that he could do *more*.

He knew he had some sort of talent... or potential... or a spark that the average person didn't. Otherwise a hot shot agent like Eddie Pryor wouldn't be so persistent about trying to sign him. And the local big timers who'd recruited him to record that silly chorus recently, they wanted him too. But was his choice only between cranking out club hits in town, or to take a leap of faith into the arms of a shifty white man whose agenda Clyde didn't really know?

Just then the TV caught his eye as it cut to some urgent news report. A lady holding a microphone was in a massive building, and people were running all around her in a panic. The camera panned to show others on the floor weeping.

"We're here," the woman said, "inside the Mall of Absolution, which is home to the mysterious Church of Modestianity. Normally members of the press are granted only limited access, but today an unprecedented event has taken place."

A man in a blue robe ran up and took the woman's microphone into his hands. He said breathlessly, "They're saying the Prescient One was responsible for the HRA hack! They came in, blew apart his sanctuary, and now he's gone! What will become of us?" He dropped the microphone and ran off.

Clyde leaned in and listened to the details of what had happened.

The reporter was back on, saying, "...this may be the last, and biggest, of the sweeping net of arrests that have reined in the Sentinels of Jubilee, the rogue group which claimed responsibility for infiltrating the MARVIN supercomputer back in early October..."

Then came a brief biography of the Prescient One, alter ego of former game developer and ousted HRA system designer Scott Cullen. "...overnight success who transformed from hard-partying playboy into an enigmatic philosopher dressed in teal, who now preaches his own reactionary brand to thousands of followers desperate for answers in these complicated and troubled times."

Clyde muted the TV. Suddenly he sensed the possibility of a third way forward for himself. A small, calculated pivot he could make. Because this man they were talking about on the TV, he too had become famous unexpectedly, and ultimately chose to "do his own thing" by creating a platform to share his beliefs.

But what do I believe. Or know, really?

This Cullen guy had been tapped into what was going on for years before he made his big choice. Would Clyde have to navigate the waters within the music industry for a while before finally seeing the personal path that fit who he was?

In a way, he was groping to *endure* as the Beneficiary who had once spoken so effectively for other Beneficiaries. But were his blind spots or lack of life experience too great an obstacle? Clyde hadn't been groomed to face the public the way that lifelong actors and politicians were.

Did he even want the responsibility of helping people just because they shared his skin color? All that deep history to think about, but he was barely sixteen years old. Maybe what he wanted was simply not to be trapped, or pigeon-holed as one thing or another.

Clyde smiled. *Pigeon*-holed. Like Nolan, who was also reinventing himself. Growing. Maturing. Trying to leave the questionable aspects of his past behind.

All of these older guys that Clyde knew had *stories*. Nolan living overseas, doing God-knows-what for the military. Sylicon and D-Eel with kids all over the place. This Prescient dude designing video games and inventing a religion. But Clyde…

He just wrote one song and then the world had opened up to him. Maybe that was too easy, not the way it was supposed to be for anyone. It was called "success," but he didn't have the callouses or past disappointments to make it feel like more than a dream.

But you couldn't go back and reverse engineer any of that. He'd just never know what it felt like to bang your head against the wall for years hoping for a breakthrough—as Nolan had tried to explain to him. He also didn't have that taste of betrayal on his tongue which had driven Scott Cullen insane—and then turned him from an ally of Beneficiaries into an enemy saboteur.

But, Clyde thought, this Church of Modestianity didn't come across as super anti-Reparations. He'd heard a little in the past about their weird rituals and funky costumes. They seemed more interested in hiding away and dancing around than fighting the government.

Clyde turned the volume back on when he saw a large, round black head fill the TV screen.

"…with the Reverend Matthias G. Witherspoon," the reporter was saying. "He's been visiting the Mall while on sabbatical from his own *Christian* church back in Ohio. Now, sir, you say you were actually meeting personally with the Prescient One when he was taken away?"

"Yes, ma'am," Matthias said, wiping dusty beads of perspiration from his temple. "We were in deep discussion about fate and life's challenges."

"So," the woman continued, "as a Beneficiary yourself, I have to ask, what are your thoughts knowing now that you were having a heart-to-heart with one of the alleged masterminds behind the hack that nearly crippled the HRA?"

Witherspoon shook his head angrily. "Y'all just don't get it. This man is thinking on a higher level! Beneficiaries… Debtors… who cares? We've all got so much work to do—on ourselves, our society, how we're going to live… Not just with each other—white, black, yellow, brown—but with all those ones and zeroes that are tracking us and judging us more harshly than any God I ever spoke to. Do you catch what I'm sayin'? It's not enough to *repent* anymore! But, do we *retreat* into the shadows, or *retaliate* viciously against this surveillance state? America, will you *recoil* in horror at the tech monster we've let loose, or—"

The reporter yanked her microphone away. "Thank you, uh, Reverend Witherspoon, for your comments. We've got to move along and speak with other Modestians…"

Clyde shut off the TV. He really needed to think now. There was something about this business at the Mall that electrified him. He sensed that… it was all so much bigger than how his mind had perceived the world only minutes ago.

The Prescient One was not just a guy sitting in his apartment writing beats and tossing them out into the ether, like a fisherman casting a line with no bait attached. But Clyde had gone that route, and it was a preposterous miracle that he not only got a nibble, but had in fact caught a giant whale with the song "Fly So High." The least he could do right now was seize upon that gift of fate by making a firm life decision. Because he finally felt like he had, maybe not *all* the information, but still a much better perspective on things.

If that Prescient fellow could go from computer nerd in a dorm room to one day offering salvation to all kinds of people, then Clyde figured there was no telling what he himself might be able to do with his own bigger ideas down the road.

But which ideas? Clyde didn't even know! But that was okay. It was time for him to get more professional as a musician, and start clearing out those blind spots.

"Okay, LA," he said to himself, "think you ready for DJC?"

22. SECRET THRILL

Chris had just run out for a quick double-errand—walk the dogs around the block after the long car ride home from Maine, as well as pick up to-go coffees for himself and Kate—so he was more than surprised to see her *repacking* her suitcase on the bed when he got back.

"Are you leaving me?" he asked jokingly while handing over her drink, but still feeling a touch of fear deep beneath his words.

She smiled, saying, "No, but duty calls!"

"In and out just like that, jeez. Back to DC then?"

Kate turned and reached into a closet, saying with a sigh, "I'm afraid things have become a bit more urgent than they were before."

"More than twenty minutes ago?"

"Apparently!" Kate removed two blouses from their hangers. "I can't pinpoint it, but something in the air really has people shook up lately."

Chris darted his eyes around the room. "So, um, where are they sending you?"

"Jamaica."

"*Jamaica?* I'm pretty sure they were a British colony."

"I know, I know. But we've got the infrastructure. It's time to help the UK set up offices, install document scanners, get their system online and repaying some debts."

"Oh," Chris said softly. "So how long are you going for?"

Kate stepped into the bathroom and unzipped a toiletry bag, then began placing items from the counter and medicine cabinet inside.

"For… a while…" She couldn't resist a smile. "Yeah, I'm really helping them do this thing!"

"So the trip's open-ended?" Chris sat on the bed.

"Jamaica's not the only country on my itinerary, either. What I don't know is if the HRA will have me come home in between, or just puddle jump."

Chris popped the cover off his coffee and drank from the lip of the cup. He said, "Kate, I know this is what you always wanted, but remember all that talk about starting a family? Does it just get pushed back, like a rescheduled flight?"

Kate looked up, then stepped closer and gave him a light kiss. "Are you saying it was something you wanted now, too?"

"We kind of let my parents know, right? I mean, I've had plenty of time to think, especially with you being so busy at work."

"I know. I'm sorry."

"But this, what I'll be doing while you're gone… holding it all together… what exactly is the point? For the Beneficiaries? For social justice? For the president? I just feel like I need more of an incentive than any of that… or whatever the next job title you get turns out to be."

Kate's eyes widened. "You want *more*… or are you asking me to make a choice?"

"I don't know," Chris said. "It's not even that I want something *else*, but whatever this life is right now is not *working*. Something's off, out of phase. And I just don't know if I need a screwdriver or a sledgehammer to fix it."

Kate pulled away slowly. "Well," she said brightly as she put on a smile, "we certainly do have a way of leaving things on a cliffhanger. But I really have to run. The car's picking me up in fifteen minutes. And Chris… I can't help but suspect that once I'm in the whirl of all this overseas business, that our conversation tonight won't be at the forefront of my thoughts. But *you'll* still be brooding. And I don't want that for you—for us."

Chris was silent for a moment. The room felt heavy in the stillness.

"I guess just try to call me when you can," he said. "I'll get your bags when you're ready."

He walked out of the room.

Kate stood there absently for a moment. As eager as she had been to get back into the swing of life after an unusually quiet car ride home, she was also secretly thrilled when that phonSe call came in telling her to pack her things for Jamaica.

Now, after the latest exchange with Chris, she realized that some of this very same tension had been present during their trip. An evasive moodiness in his demeanor which she couldn't just pass off as the fatigue that came from dealing with one's family in close quarters.

Kate folded each article of clothing and placed it neatly into the suitcase. She watched the accents of her machine-made diamond engagement ring reflect vividly in the room's soft light.

Suddenly she wanted nothing more than to be out of this apartment and on the road again.

23. PREDATOR AND PREY

"Got a light?"

"Yeah, sure. Here."

The burly man reached into the pocket of his black canvas jacket and pulled out a silver Zippo.

"A classic," the other man said, lighting up and inspecting the chrome piece before handing it back.

"Yup. My dad got it back in the day."

"Nice. What time do you guys go on?"

"We're next. You, uh, you a fan?"

"Oh yeah! Never too old to rock, right?"

"Haha, I'm trying. What's your name, by the way?"

The first man held out his hand and smiled. "Marcus," he said. "Nice to meet you."

"Likewise. Glenn. Alright, I'm gonna head back in."

FBI Special Agent Marcus Young watched him pass through the front entrance, then gave his own cigarette one long last drag before tossing it down into the street. Real tobacco smokes were a rare treat these days.

But, Marcus mused, he had already encountered a number of throwbacks during this stakeout on the life of Glenn Murray. Old cars, old combat boots, and tonight an old flip-top lighter.

Marcus, tasked with collaring this suspected SOJ spy, had followed him down from Philadelphia to this dive bar in Manassas, Virginia. Glenn's band Bleeding the Aggregate was performing tonight, and then—perhaps he would rendezvous with other conspirators to damage HRA infrastructure.

During all his years as an FBI agent, Marcus Young tried to get as close to his quarry as possible. Was it in order to better know the man, or just some kind of sick personal thrill? Part of the lifelong process of understanding the criminal mind—or was he testing the effectiveness of his own facade?

Either way, Marcus had felt compelled to come down from his crow's nest of surveillance and meet Glenn in person. He'd outfitted himself with a faded leather jacket and torn jeans, then even painted his fingernails black in an effort to blend in with the rough-edged crowd that attended these punk rock concerts.

He stepped inside the venue, paid the modest cover charge, and ordered a beer at the bar. A small melee of bodies was churning a chaotic circle in front of the stage, where a high-energy trio was blasting away.

This was the sort of tangible data that you could only get by playing chameleon and inhabiting the world of your target. The two-man team that was hanging back in an unmarked car couldn't *feel* what was going on in the way that Marcus did right now. Not only were surveillance cameras and microphones limited in what they could monitor—Marcus wanted to *taste* his prey.

The bass player on stage sent a searing and gravelly "Yeah!" into his microphone, then held the yell until his voice slowly died away.

Marcus felt the impact of that howl in his core. This

was why he *loved* going undercover and being right there in the midst of real life. All of a sudden the Mall of Absolution felt very far away, and in turn his life as a Modestian… Had he merely bought into that role too deeply?

These were not the types of thoughts that Special Agent Marcus Young could afford to have right now. He was supposed to be a hardcore-punk music fan out having a good time on a Saturday night. He picked up his neglected beer and quickly drank half of it down, then set the pint glass onto the bar loudly. No one paid him any mind.

Half an hour later, after Glenn's band had set up on stage, Marcus made his way into the crowd of sixty-plus that was in attendance. He stood safely away from the slam-dancers up front, but was still close enough to take in Glenn's visceral performance.

The canvas jacket was off now, and pasty freckled arms were strangling a silver-capped microphone as he unleashed a raspy wail. Then Glenn moved left, planting his boot onto a speaker and pointing menacingly into the crowd. He tilted his head back and roared, with his face and beard changing colors under the flashing stage lights.

"Another… changing of the guard! Why bother… the plan marches on!"

Who was this man? Marcus asked himself. A talented performer with the kind of charisma that demanded you pay attention. The way that Glenn took possession of the stage, surely his band couldn't just be a cover for the SOJ activities. Besides, Marcus had seen several people wearing Bleeding the Aggregate t-shirts, and the small merchandise table was doing respectable business.

As the enveloping assault of blistering crust-punk

continued around him, Marcus wondered if this Glenn Murray knew something that he didn't. Was this imposing man not only righteous, but *right* in his anger toward the HRA?

Marcus himself had always felt mostly ambivalent towards the Reparations movement. Being three-quarters black and coming from a family of educated professionals, he had lived a privileged life that was anchored in constant work and striving. His friendships were based on the sports he played, the college he and his wealthy classmates attended.

So the HRA and its spray-and-pray method of dispensing funds to anyone who happened to fall into the Beneficiary class—this as a philosophical approach just seemed alien to him. His family had already risen; he didn't need anyone else's help.

As for his brothers and sisters in the so-called black community... Marcus felt more palpable kinship as a member of the law enforcement fraternity. No matter a person's race, creed, or gender—when you put on that badge, you were all working toward the organization's common goals.

Just like when Marcus was an individual player on his college baseball *team*. And as he had later become one small but valued part of the living, breathing, growing idea that was the Church of Modestianity.

Marcus suddenly fought his way back toward the bar. He ordered a shot of whiskey and sent it down, then motioned for another even while knowing that this was going a step beyond the role he was supposed to be playing. Have one or two beers throughout the night, fine. But don't get wasted drunk and risk exposing yourself...

"They don't realize it yet," Marcus muttered. "They don't see what's at stake."

"What's that?" the bartender called out over the din, looking up from the drink he was mixing a few feet away.

"Nothing," Marcus said with a wave. "Same old shit."

"Ha, don't I know it!" The bartender shook his head with a sheepish grin, then walked away carrying a glass in each hand.

Marcus leaned onto the bar and looked back at the stage. Glenn was in full command up there—confident, surging, completely in his element.

Then he looked down at the black polish on his fingernails. A few tones lighter and he'd be no different than the Prescient One. Just another costumed man playing out a role, hiding or reacting…

"Lost! Lost!" Glenn growled into the microphone.

Marcus looked at him again, then at all the people in the club. Everyone *was* lost. But still on alert, always seeking the voice or the idea that would set them back on a good path.

A sick feeling rose up from Marcus's stomach. It wasn't the alcohol or tobacco though. It was dread. Because if his intuition was correct, he would have to arrest Glenn Murray—the very man who seemed so sure of himself, of the truth, and of how things ought to be.

And if this was the type of person that the government wanted to lock up, then Special Agent Marcus Young was almost ashamed to be a part of the net that was slowly closing in to silence Glenn's plaintive voice.

He closed his tab at the bar and walked back out into the chilly night. He would surely see Glenn Murray again sometime after the show—all that remained was the how and when.

24. FALLING AWAY

As he packed a work bag in the silence of his home office, Chris Donohugh wondered if he would ever again find a way to really shine. The near future in his mind's eye didn't seem to hold much promise of that, not for someone who had spent a lifetime putting the needs of others ahead of his own.

He pictured Kate seven months pregnant, arriving home for a quick weekend in the city, then back down to DC doing her critical work. He of course would be available to accommodate her at all times. And later, when the baby came, maybe even be expected to close up shop on his life in New York City and relocate to Northern Virginia. Because he couldn't very well live apart from his newborn, or leave so much responsibility to his in-laws.

And yet... fatherhood! His own little child to teach how to ride a bike. There would be birthdays, with Kate bringing out the cake... He would be taking pictures to capture the moment... But perhaps deep in his breast, that one secret betrayal would live on intertwined with the frustrations and disappointments that lingered.

Chris left the apartment with the pawn-shop laptop stowed in his carry bag. He took the subway on a circuitous route, stepping off at random stations and once even letting his desired train pass by, before finally ending up in the area of Central Park.

He bought a coffee with cash from a bakery that faced an open courtyard, then took a seat on the semi-enclosed patio that had gas heaters. He opened the laptop and sipped his drink while it booted up—just another city dweller getting some work done while out and about.

"Dude," he typed. "Got some bad news. Big new project came up at work. Not sure I'm gonna be able to do any music for a while after all. Hope you can make something out of what we already jammed on."

Chris sent the message. Gently, he pressed the laptop lid down. Hopefully Glenn would accept that this was the end of the road.

He gazed outside through the unfurled clear plastic that housed the patio. A man in a navy pea coat was looking at him from the pavement outside. A hand went to the ear. Now the lips moved briefly. The other hand fidgeted inside a pocket.

Chris felt his body clench to near rigor mortis. Had he finally been caught? Were government agents converging for some horrific raid in broad daylight that dozens of cameras would record? Was the all-too-public scandal which had played out in his mind fifty times actually about to unfold?

Chris understood what he had to do. Casually pack up his things, then meander back inside the cafe to dispose of his cup, just like any other responsible citizen on his way to the restroom. He would next dash into the kitchen and look for a way out back. If someone was waiting for him there—

Suddenly the man standing out front began to nod his head, then pointed a finger in Chris's direction. Chris heard a firework explode inside his head as the man took a step forward...

Then in stunned silence, and with vivid tunnel vision, Chris saw a woman come into view from the left. The man turned toward her and gave a big smile as he leaned over the stroller she was pushing. The hand that was in the pocket slid out and flashed a small toy, then disappeared behind the stroller's canopy.

The couple embraced, then slowly walked away and out of view.

Chris stared down with unfocused eyes at the little table for nearly a minute. Slowly his heart rate dropped back to normal. He rose, put on his coat, packed the laptop away, and finally walked out the bakery's front door into the gray wintry day.

He was safe.

But something very hollow and troubling stayed with him. He had nowhere to go. No pressing work to do. No one to meet at home later in the afternoon— except two hungry dogs. His guy friends were all at normal day jobs...

Chris felt a longing that was encapsulated by the word *Kate*, but he couldn't shake the feeling that it came from a position of weakness or neediness. Whereas, if she was even thinking of him... He was taken for granted. An underling serving the boss's needs. A knot that just had to be massaged the right way so that she could get what she wanted.

Now he really didn't know what to do. He couldn't very well reopen the laptop and tell Glenn he was back on board helping the Sentinels bring the HRA crashing to its knees. But he also couldn't reach out to Kate—

and risk coming across as the lonely spouse
pathetically hounding the all-star who was busy
making waves.

Chris turned his brain off and started walking
through Central Park. If only these trees, whose leaves
were dying and falling away, could impart some of
their timeless stoicism to help him endure this crisis.
Because at the moment, he felt dangerously close to
losing himself altogether.

25. MORE PRIMITIVE

"But my good lady, perhaps we need more than simply money to heal our wounds. If indeed the white man used to rule over us, and now you are here to make amends... Should you not also send Caucasian laborers or servants to achieve this noble aim?"

Kate Donohugh stared incredulously across the walnut desk. Jamaica's Minister of Finance and the Public Service, the Honorable Thomas Howard Nelson, was smiling sardonically at her with arms folded over his stomach. Portraits of a dozen national heroes were mounted on the walls of this stately office.

"But sir," she said, "Reparations is primarily meant to settle the books. People must still be involved in their own lives, and responsible for shaping their future destiny."

"No, ma'am," Nelson said. "You do not get to set the terms of your concession. Not if it is to be seen as done in good faith. If you truly believe that you owe us for past crimes against our people, then surely it would be a conflict of interest if you were in charge of setting the parameters, and then to also act as the executor. No?"

"Honorable minister, my government is acting as an intermediary on behalf of the United Kingdom in this matter. What would you have us do?"

"Give us control of both the funds and the operation," Minister Nelson said flatly. "Who knows the island people better than those of us who also live here?"

"Mr. Nelson," Kate said, "surely you know that's not how our charter is written. I have to follow the letter of the law."

"Man, to hell with what's on that piece of paper!" the man burst out. "That's how we were all bought and sold to begin with. Hundreds of years of evil, chronicled in great detail by these documents—and now you dare to wave a new one in front of my face?"

"With all due respect, if there weren't any surviving historical documents then there would be no Reparations to speak of at all." Kate sighed. "I *really* hate to quote one of my ideological opponents, but the Dutch politician Erich Bakker made a valid point when testifying before the United Nations last year. He noted the irony of how cultures that had a written language and kept meticulous records, they are now the ones being held accountable. Whereas more primitive people, whose traditions were often communicated orally, have no such archives to track down and—"

The man sucked at his tongue, shaking his head sadly. "And there it is," he said. "The condescension I knew would come. Even from the mouths of so-called allies, I hear it all the time. But, what am I to do? If I kick you out of my office, they will just send another in your place. And the funds will be delayed for my principled troubles."

"Minister Nelson," Kate said as she forced a smile, "may I offer a personal insight? During my several years working for the HRA, I dealt intimately with members of the public, both Beneficiaries and Debtors. This... tension we're experiencing today is just part of the process. There is *a lot* of money on the line here. And that's why this *has* to be set up so formally, because the possibility for corruption is just too great otherwise."

"Do you think I, or my people, that we are tempted to steal, Mrs. Donohugh?"

Kate pursed her lips. "I make no such assumption," she said. "Nor did I write out the policies. But I *am* here as a liaison on behalf of the President of the United States, whose staff I have worked with personally. So I'm afraid that when I tell you there are strings attached—"

"They are actually ropes?" Nelson brought his fingertips together. "Thick hemp ropes, as once used on the great sailing ships that carried away my ancestors from their beloved homeland, which they had known for thousands of years."

"If you want," Kate said slowly, "to find a metaphor in everything I say, you probably can. But I do think we should try to get some work done here. My instructions say that five facilities should be set up to begin with. And since there are primarily Beneficiaries on the island, we won't have to build new divided structures, as we did back in the US. That should definitely expedite your country receiving its funds. So for one, I'll need someone to help research where the appropriate buildings might be found."

Minister Nelson paused. "Ma'am, I don't really know if this project is something we want to be a part of."

"But I don't understand. Your government has already come into de facto agreement…"

"When I hear you talk about doing this or that, telling me I need to find people to set up offices… It sounds to me like you are trying to assert control over my country."

"That's ridiculous."

"Yes, yes, I know." The minister leaned forward onto his elbows. "To you it may seem that way. But this has been America's playbook around the world in recent times. Instead of colonists or armies or missionaries, it is organizations such as yours, and the Peace Corps before that, which send attractive young ladies into poor countries under the guise of offering assistance to the lowly brown people. But nothing ever improves! All we are left with is your footprints, your litter, and the dangerous ideas you have put into the minds of our people."

"Sir," Kate bristled, "I have devoted fifteen years of my life to helping the less fortunate, be they black, white, trans, disabled—anyone who is marginalized in any way."

Mr. Nelson stood up. "Mrs. Donohugh," he said, "I am kindly asking you to leave. This office and my country."

"Like you said, they'll just send somebody else." And as Kate began to pack up her things, she was shocked to hear herself say bitterly, "Maybe someone who isn't as… personable as me."

The minister extended his hand formally.

"Then tell your people that next time, perhaps my response won't be as civil either. Yes," he added with a chuckle, "I shall act more… *primitively*. Good day to you."

26. IT AIN'T FAIR

The limo came to pick him up at noon. When he went to grab his bags, Tyrell wouldn't let go of his leg.

Clyde patted him on the head. "It's okay, kid. I ain't going forever."

A tear ran down one of Tyrell's cheeks. He bowed his head.

"Uncle Clyde, I need you to play them games with me."

Clyde looked up at his mother and sister who were standing nearby. Octavius was out, but they'd already shared a brief and uneventful farewell the night before.

"Game time is over, for a while," he said to his nephew.

"But it ain't fair," Tyrell said, his lips quivering.

"Oh my Lord," Dawna Jenkins said, lifting her grandson up into her arms. "You don't even know how much 'it ain't fair' there is to go 'round. Now come on and be a big boy for your uncle."

Tyrell buried his face into Dawna's shoulder.

"You makin' it hard for me," Clyde said. He gently

rubbed Tyrell's back. "I'll see you soon, little man. Promise."

Myra leaned in and gave Clyde a hug. "Take care of yourself, baby brother. I'm so proud of you."

"Yeah. Do right by this boy here. He's my special buddy. You hear that, Mister Tee?"

Tyrell reached out his hand and Clyde gave it an energetic shake.

"You got to go now," Dawna said. "Don't forget about us."

"Why you say that, Mama?" Clyde gave her a big hug after Myra had taken Tyrell into her own arms. "I'll always still be me."

Dawna smiled. "In my heart you will. But now it's time to live your life. Go knock 'em dead."

The city he'd grown up in sped by on the way to the airport. After everything that had happened since the summer, all these people were still here chipping away at this game of life.

Somehow it was Clyde who had made a name for himself on the back of their suffering, and now he was leaving the cold Newark winter for a chance in sunny California. Other people did come and go from the old neighborhood, of course, but he had found a way *out*— even though for so long his heart had wanted to stick around and be with everybody.

But destiny was often just the right combination of timing and opportunity. Clyde finally understood that he would be a fool to not seize upon the DJ Clydoscope name for all it was worth right now. So he had called Eddie Pryor and told that slick LA agent what he had been waiting to hear—that Clyde was ready to play ball and go big time.

A liaison greeted Clyde when the limo pulled up to the curb at the Newark airport. This man instructed a skycap to load up Clyde's bags, then escorted him through the terminal.

At one point Clyde, who was dressed somewhat incognito hoping to avoid being spotted, paused when he saw a big sign for international departures. He stared at it for several seconds, until the liaison said, "Is something the matter, Mr. Jenkins?"

"No," Clyde said with a smile. "One step at a time."

"Very good, sir. Now, please follow me and we'll bypass those awful lines to get you on board much more quickly."

Not long afterward, Clyde was comfortably seated and awaiting takeoff. On the private jet that had been arranged by Eddie Pryor.

Clyde chuckled. By playing hard to get he had graduated from First Class to this. *And* with a flop of a second single sandwiched in between. Who else could claim that?

Probably another life lesson in there somewhere. Because only weeks ago he had been set on sticking to his guns with "Soul's Gold." Now his integrity wasn't so much being rewarded, as maybe taking a sideline to Eddie's more pressing interests.

But also, Clyde remembered seeing a lot of framed headshots on the wall at Nolan's favorite diner. They were signed by actors and singers who were all formally trained and probably quite talented, but who had just never caught a lucky break. Clyde knew he couldn't afford to squander his own good fortune.

When the little plane lifted off and popped out through the cloud cover, Clyde Jenkins had enough clarity of mind to sense that, while he might not fully know himself, it would all turn out okay. Because he was about to jump headlong into the professional arena, which would reveal to him and the world just who really was behind the DJ Clydoscope persona.

Genius? Fluke? Impostor? Or the next rising star headed for an unforgettable career?

I'm an uncle, Clyde thought. *A brother and a son. A Jenkins, forever.*

He looked out the window and contemplated the colorful sky, as his jet raced along in its quest to catch the receding sun.

27. A SHINE ON HIS SOUL

Reverend Witherspoon could not help but feel a touch of whimsical longing as he drove away from the Mall of Absolution. The people inside had given him a very special gift, yet he was now leaving them at a time of great uncertainty for the church.

The four days since the Prescient One's abduction had been filled with some of the most gut-wrenching moments of Matthias's life. The fear, pain, and confusion he saw on the once-bright faces of his Modestian friends might have brought a weaker man to despair.

But instead, Matthias Witherspoon saw this crisis as an opportunity to employ his newfound strength and clarity, as he helped shepherd many people across the bridge from shock to calm comfort. He told them to not lose hope, and look toward one another for reassurance —because God imposed setbacks not to cripple people's will, but as a challenge for them to redouble their resolve.

Yes, the Christian teachings he had shared over a

lifetime while presiding over his own church, so many of them had translated beautifully at the Mall. And perhaps, Matthias thought, this was the key to the Prescient One's success. That man hadn't simply created a new religion out of whole cloth—because as quirky as many of its surface features were, everything in Modestianity's core was grounded in the realities of human life.

As Matthias came to understand while sitting in on the nightly mapmaking sessions, the religion initially sprang up as a *reactionary* belief system—society caught in the manic throes of twenty-first-century life —but had since opened itself up to any and all forms of *inspiration* that might further launch the souls of its people into fulfillment and joy.

Thus it was with a bittersweet swirl of emotions that Reverend Witherspoon decided it was time to depart for home. His own flock had been without a leader for two weeks now. And truth be told, the controversial Sunday sermon he delivered just prior to the election had sent a fracture through his church. Those members who viewed services as a kind of social event were appalled that Matthias would invoke so much fire and brimstone, let alone aim any of that judgmental wrath at the congregation itself. Some of them up and quit, while others demanded the preacher either recant or resign his post.

Thankfully for Matthias, about a third of his followers resonated with his admonishment to hold themselves more accountable in the game of life. This group refused to let their voices be drowned out. They told the complainers that the purpose of a church was to challenge oneself, and not simply serve as a venue to strut around in fancy suits and floral dresses.

Under the dark shadow of this rift, Witherspoon had

announced his intention to take a leave of absence so that he might find the solution to all of their woes. Each side sheepishly agreed to a temporary ceasefire until the reverend's return.

And now he was going home.

Fortified in ways that he couldn't have imagined, but certainly hoped to be. Tested by the unforeseen trauma of a special ops team descending upon the Mall in a stealth raid. Then feeling the weight of oppression in subsequent days, as other law enforcement members patrolled the corridors.

And ultimately, walking away with a shine on his soul courtesy of these idealistic Modestian believers and their resilient spirit. As the spark of life returned to their eyes, and confidence in the church's strength was reaffirmed—that was the moment Matthias knew he could leave them in good conscience.

The remaining church leaders had in fact called a general assembly, where they played a previously recorded speech by the Prescient One entitled "Continuing the Covenant." He declared that he would soon depart from the Mall—either by choice or by force—but was confident that the end result would only bring more glory to the Church of Modestianity.

Initial shock at their leader's announcement—that he actually *planned* or *expected* to leave them—soon gave way to faithful acceptance, because he always seemed to have a forward-thinking plan. They took heart in his commitment to always act as their guide. Therefore, if he ever disappeared from sight, it was not because he had abandoned them.

Matthias hated to see their leader's name dragged through the mud, particularly after his own enlightening discussion with the man. The reverend was still processing the allegation that the Prescient

One was *also* that masked man who had delivered the Sentinels of Jubilee's staggering existential warning nearly two months ago.

Witherspoon chuckled to himself. Yes, he still was and would always be a Christian, but in this instance he chose to humbly defer to the Prescient One and trust in the other man's penetrating insights.

In the meantime, he had a great deal of work to do back home in Akron, Ohio. The first order of business was to repair the splinter inside his church before it turned into an all-out civil war. Next he would begin investing resources to strengthen his local community, just as he had vowed to do in that contentious Sunday sermon.

If the Church of Modestianity was now experiencing its first dark night of the soul, then his own people had already endured a torturous half-millennium. Matthias vowed that he would work tirelessly for his black brothers and sisters so that they might heal, rebuild, and find common ground. None of them could afford to face the future with bitterness toward one another.

Because as Matthias had sensed in a chillingly prescient vision of his own, neither fork in the Reparations highway boded well for black folk in America. Any decline or dilution of the HRA would be painful enough, but still worse... If the Reparations movement planned to spread worldwide in order to keep itself relevant as a brand, then surely the original Beneficiaries would be forgotten in the expanding gold rush. He would have to mentally prepare his people for all of these contingencies now.

As the Reverend Matthias G. Witherspoon drove along the cold interstate heading south, he thought he saw a glint of the Prescient One smiling at him in the rear view mirror. He began to hum to himself as he plotted out the next sermon he would deliver to the members of his church.

"My people, my people. It is *good* to be back home once again. But now it's time for all of us to get to work…"

28. SUDDENLY

Chris Donohugh found himself almost giddy as he scrambled to clean up the mess he'd created throughout the apartment in the four days since Kate had left town. Now she was suddenly on her way back—something bad had happened, but her messages as to exactly what had all been vague. The only thing she would confirm was that it had nothing to do with her health.

He was amazed at how quickly all of the emotions that had been crushing him simply rinsed away at the very thought of his wife coming home early. He allowed himself to savor the feeling, and didn't worry about how long until she went back out on the road.

Instead he cranked up his stereo system and had a "heavy metal cleaning day." This had once been the tradition among Chris and his college roommates, and it was an incredible way to quickly get the household chores done. Wicked-fast drummers set the pace, a bunch of angry singers kept you on task, and whammy-bar-powered guitar solos inspired heroic acts of sweeping and scrubbing. And today, two dogs also provided backing vocals.

When Kate arrived home that evening, Chris was sitting on the couch with legs crossed on the ottoman. His heart and the Corgis all jumped at the same instant.

He entered the front hall just as she stooped down to receive the dogs' love. She looked up—eyes and face so tired—but still the beautiful girl he'd fallen in love with all those years ago.

"Hi, babe!" he called as he rushed over to her. "I'm so glad you're home."

Kate stood up, dropping wearily into his open arms. "I am most definitely home. Whew!"

Chris carried her bags into the apartment as she slipped off her jacket and pulled out a dining room chair.

"Oh... my... goodness," Kate said. She rubbed her face with her hands. "I am one tired girl."

"And thirsty too?" Chris asked. He stepped into the kitchen and removed a bottle of wine from the pantry shelf.

"Could be!" Kate extended her hand to receive it, then inspected the label. "Ooh. Milton Ravine... From 'twenty-five? I didn't know we had this!"

"Nope." Chris smiled. "I picked it up this afternoon."

"Aw... Please, do the honors. I only have enough energy left to lift a stem."

"Certainly, m'lady."

Chris made a silly show of formally presenting the Merlot with a dish towel draped over his forearm. He mumbled in a French accent as he removed the cork and set it on the table. Kate played along in her role of snooty restaurant patron, first by swirling the sample pour doubtfully, then sipping and finally approving with a dignified nod.

When a red drop of the wine ran down along the outside edge of her glass and clung to the lip of the base for an unbearable second, Kate stuck out a finger to dab it, then brought it up to her tongue. They both burst out laughing.

Chris sat down at the corner seat beside her and smiled. He said, "So, to what disaster do I owe this surprise visit?"

Kate assumed a haughty formal tone and said, "The Honorable Minister Thomas Howard Nelson, of Such-and-Such Department, has requested the presence of fifteen hundred white butlers and field laborers. In addition, of course, to the funds already promised. Now Mr. Donohugh, with your admirable corkage skills, would you be interested in such an opportunity?"

"What—I mean, *what?!*" Chris said.

Kate gulped some wine, shaking her head with a smile as she said, "I really should savor this more, but I think I need to get drunk."

"Go for it! We've got something cheaper I can open too, or… pour you a shot?"

"No, no. I'll ease into this. I was just… so looking forward to being home! And now I'm here, so… yeah, no rush anymore."

"Great," Chris said, sipping from his own glass. "Wow, this *is* good."

"Yup. So," Kate said, easing back into her chair. "The first overseas trip didn't go too well. So poorly in fact, that the folks down in DC decided to send me home while they figure out what the hell happened."

"Well, what the hell *did* happen?"

"When I got back," Kate mused, "some of the folks at the White House clued me in to a few of their… regional insights. Maybe they were just trying to make me feel better, and not think that I failed them."

"Enlighten me about these insights."

"You've heard the expression 'island time' before. What I encountered is what Eileen's people call 'island pride.' The leaders see their populations as a tight-knit community, so they don't like it when big countries show up and tell them how to run their lives."

"Okay," Chris nodded, "I can totally see that. But with so many countries out there to potentially work with, how did this all get so screwed up? Did no one in DC predict that this might happen?"

"Chris, my darling," Kate said, spinning the stem of her glass between thumb and forefinger, "that is what we in government simply refer to as 'the price of doing bureaucracy.' "

He smiled. "I'll stay in the private sector then. And you, meanwhile, need to get some rest. You look exhausted."

"I am." Kate tilted her head. "What about you? How were you holding up?"

"Eh… Not a lot going on with work. Clients always slow down around holiday time. But I did restring my Gibson and start messing around trying to remember how to play."

"Oh yeah? That's great! My husband, the thirty-something rocker. Because punk will never die, am I right?"

"Never!" Chris declared, grabbing the wine bottle and raising it triumphantly. He also took the opportunity to refill their glasses.

"Oh, God," Kate said breezily. "We do make a cute couple, don't we?"

She smiled at him with such sweetness that Chris thought he might do a backflip. He heard himself say, "I bet our kid would be cute, too."

Now it was Kate's turn to contemplate spontaneous

gymnastics. But instead, she leaned in and planted a slow, moist kiss onto his lips.

"I want to do better," she whispered.

"Yeah?" Chris said. "What… how do you mean?"

"You're my world. Which means you're more important than the rest of the world."

"Is that why you came home?"

"No, they really did send me back. But it's going to be my decision to stay."

"*Stay?* As in… no more Eileen?"

Kate lifted her glass as she slung her other arm over the chairback. "Now look here, fella," she said with a film-noir affect. "That Jeffries-Lao dame is only gonna be in office til 'thirty-two. I hope—no, I *expect* you to stick around for a lot longer than that. You hear?"

Chris's eyes began to water as some horrendous pit in his stomach fell away. He felt lighter and freer than he had in years.

He flipped the dish towel back onto his arm, wiggled his whiskers, and resumed the role of French waiter. He said, "But of course, madam. Who else would keep your wine glass full?"

Kate and Chris Donohugh reached out and held each other's hands in silence.

29. GOING UNDERGROUND

"Where the hell is he going?"

FBI Special Agent Marcus Young had asked himself this question aloud half a dozen times in the hour since Glenn Murray had pulled onto the highway and begun a winding drive through hilly Blue Ridge Mountain country.

Marcus's two partners had split off to tail the man who had met with Glenn earlier at a gas station in Charleston, West Virginia. By all appearances, Glenn was just a guy picking up an old SUV that needed repairs. He had then driven off alone—his tour van and bandmates were nowhere around—and Marcus felt in his gut that the chase was finally on!

But every mile Glenn drove on Route 119 in a southwesterly direction took him further away from cities or any of the military and government facilities indicated on Marcus's official map. This was what perplexed him so much. If Glenn was en route to his next act of sabotage, Marcus wondered, what could he do in a region of mostly farmland and tree-capped hills?

Marcus had to keep his distance now. Traffic had been sparse on the curvy highway, and after exiting a short while ago, Glenn had since made a series of turns onto smaller and smaller country roads. Finally Marcus was forced to stay even further back when Glenn veered onto a bumpy dirt road, and use the dust kicked up by the SUV's large tires to keep track of where he was. All Marcus could hope was that Glenn didn't check his mirrors and take note of Marcus's own swirling dust.

Suddenly the wispy brown chimney stopped rising up about a quarter mile in the distance. Marcus pulled his own car off to the side of the road. He put on his coat, then trotted briskly in the direction of where Glenn had come to a stop. His right hand subconsciously tapped against the .40 cal Glock 23 handgun on his hip. He hoped he wouldn't have to use it.

The gray Toyota Sequoia was sitting a few feet off the road in a patch of craggy plant life that was in the process of entering its dormant winter state. Marcus scanned the scene quickly—one cluster of trees leading away, but not nearly thick enough for Glenn to have run into without still being seen now. Otherwise the space was wide open, with wisps of tall grass and a number of bushes dotting the area. There were no buildings in sight.

Marcus suddenly wondered if Glenn had come all the way out here to commit suicide. He unholstered his pistol and made a wide arc around the trunk, checking inside from a distance to see if there were any human forms inside.

Once he had ascertained that both front seats were empty, Marcus sprinted up against the left rear panel and peered in through the tinted windows. He was perplexed to see the entire back seating and storage areas filled with the kind of supplies one would take on a family camping trip.

"A real big fan, huh?"

Marcus felt his heart surge with a rush of adrenaline as he swung around and raised his gun in one quick motion. He saw Glenn standing thirty feet away. Same black canvas jacket. Burgundy wool cap. Hands raised out to the side. Both empty.

Marcus blinked, exhaled heavily through his mouth.

"What the hell are you doing out here, Glenn?"

"Took me a second to place you," Glenn responded. "Who do you work for?"

Marcus lowered his weapon slightly, but kept both hands on it, ready to aim and fire in an instant.

"FBI Special Agent Marcus Young. Mr. Murray, I have reason to believe you are engaged in illegal activities on behalf of the Sentinels of Jubilee. Including but not limited to sabotaging the Historical Reparations Administration."

"Am I suspect then?" Glenn said calmly.

"Yes, you *are* a suspect! Now don't play games with me. What is the purpose of your travel today, sir?"

Glenn made a motion to lower his arms. "May I?"

"Yes, but keep 'em where I can see 'em. Now start talking. I noticed a lot of supplies in the back of this truck. But your band isn't around. What are you up to?"

Marcus saw Glenn's face soften, heard him say, "It ain't what you think, man."

"I don't know anything yet," Marcus snapped. "Lay it out for me, nice and clear."

Glenn Murray chuckled. "You know, I don't want to die. But this is about more than me."

"Glenn! I'm not here to hurt you. Just tell me what's going on. Who or what is out here that would make you bring all this stuff?"

The bearded man looked down, stamped his feet. He said, "You took an oath to the Constitution, right?"

"That's correct," Marcus said. "The United States Uniformed Services Oath of Office. What does that have to do with all that's going on here?"

"Because," Glenn said, "I drove out all this way to deliver these supplies to American citizens. And whatever laws I may have broken in the past, I can't let you put any of them in danger."

"Danger?!" Marcus was exasperated. "Are they all Sentinel fugitives too?"

"Not in the least. Jesus Christ," Glenn sighed. "They're just people."

"But where?" Marcus took one hand off his pistol and waved it around. "There's nothing for miles."

Glenn took a step forward. "Come on, I'll show you."

The next few minutes were a blur for Special Agent Marcus Young. Getting into the Toyota with Glenn. Agreeing to leave his electronic devices back in the other car. The steep, winding drive directly onto one of the nearby hills that dotted the countryside. Pulling off onto a slender path, before stopping and backing up close to the mouth of a cave that dipped sharply down into the earth.

"Okay," Glenn said. "Let's unload."

"*What?* Here?!"

Marcus stepped out of the truck, his head swooning, then saw several people emerge from the cave.

"It's alright," he heard Glenn say, but wasn't sure if those words were intended for himself or the others.

For the next ten minutes he helped unload the truck in silence, handing cases of canned food and toiletries to the men and boys who hustled back down into the cave's entrance. Heavy trash bags were then brought out and placed inside the vehicle.

Marcus saw Glenn exchange a few final words with one of the men, then motion to get back in the truck. As they pulled forward down the slope, Marcus turned back and saw that several of the helpers were obscuring the SUV's tracks with brooms.

"So," Glenn said finally, "are you a patriot or a subversive now?"

"I don't understand," Marcus said. "Who were those people?"

"Guys who just needed to get their families away from it all."

Marcus was stunned. "Did you say… families? Glenn, how many people are inside that cave right now?"

"That one? Oh, about twenty-five or thirty."

"You mean there are *other* groups living in *other* caves?"

"Yep." Glenn tapped his fingers along the top of the steering wheel.

"My god… But why?!"

"We all fight for what we believe—or love—in our own way. There's a storm overhead in this country, and they're trying to ride it out in safety, I guess."

Marcus experienced a sudden flashback to the days when he was living incognito as Bill Evans at the Church of Modestianity. There too he had heard talk of storm clouds and taking shelter. As they now rounded a curve and his own car came into view, he found himself desperate for air.

"We need to talk," Marcus said as he spilled out onto the side of the dirt road.

Glenn leaned back against the right side of the hood and waited for Marcus to compose himself. Finally the

FBI man said, "So you're telling me people are hiding away from Reparations, surveillance, or whatever... in caves all over the state?"

"All over the country, probably," Glenn remarked.

"But why?" Marcus pleaded. "It's just a tax. It can't go on forever—and they can't survive like that for long."

"I don't think they're doing it for the money." Glenn lit a cigarette with the Zippo, then offered one to Marcus. "It's about capitulation. A lot of us are waking up to the fact that no amount of concession will ever satisfy... whatever you want to call the mindset that's behind this Reparations movement."

Marcus took a drag on his own cigarette and tossed the lighter back. He said, "Glenn, I've got a file on you going all the way back to when you were thirteen years old spraying anarchy symbols on street signs. Nowhere did I see anything about your life that said 'right wing'."

Glenn nodded. "I was always so sure about how things were supposed to be. Just like everyone else is, nowadays. Wanna know why? Because we're *all* extremists on the inside. With me, the tide must have secretly shifted at some point, and where I stood went from idealist to... what, being an insurgent?"

Marcus felt a chill ripple through his body. He said, "Just a few years ago, they held parades because people thought they were taking part in the end of history. *They were sure of it*. But now... I don't know. Is the beginning of our own version of the Russian Revolution actually what's happening?"

The air was getting cooler, the shadows slowly lengthening in the mid-afternoon light of this autumn day.

"You know how it always starts?" Glenn asked. "The unraveling, that is? The path, it begins with everyone saying that they're just trying to help. The HRA. You cops. Even me," he added ruefully. "You know, volunteer work, lyrics with a 'message.' Then somehow I found myself involved with... hmm... those other things. It's funny how we all justify to ourselves what we're doing. Because now it's not simply, 'I'm good and my enemies are evil.' No, the wording got more complex, but human nature hasn't changed. By saying that you're 'fighting for people' or 'building bridges'... You can get away with *anything* using phrases like that as cover—even excuse when your equally righteous allies give in to temptation worse than the average person."

"So you think it's lack of scruples all the way down?" Marcus asked. "Then why does anyone lift a finger?"

"And not also pick up a sword when they do?" Glenn said. "Beats me."

They both smiled briefly.

Marcus said, "So tell me, if everyone thinks they're the good guy, and nobody's actually running a secret genocide program out of their food pantry... Where does it all go wrong? What's the glitch that makes everybody crazy, so that right now you and I are out here, instead of doing something simple and above-board back in our communities?"

"You're asking *me* for answers?" Glenn thumped a fist against the side of the truck. "I was screaming about the same things for fifteen years before I finally realized that maybe I had blinders on. Didn't see the whole picture."

"How so?" Marcus folded his arms.

"I mean, there's just so much going on behind the scenes that you'll never be privy to. Everywhere. As for me personally, I hate to think that my scene—punk, hardcore—we're just a steam valve that keeps concerned people distracted. Compartmentalized. Not taking action. Thinking *small*."

Marcus said, "I don't really know as much about your musical world as I let on the last time we met. Can you explain it more?"

"Alright," Glenn said. "Take capitalism, or war. Couple of buzzwords that every kid who sees a chopped-down rainforest or flattened city can write songs about. But anyone who works in those industries, they all truly think they're helping. Making their family proud. Providing materials for the village. Fighting against evil."

"Capturing the saboteur?" Marcus said, raising his eyebrows.

"Yeah." Glenn chuckled nervously. "But you can't really put that kind of nuance into my style of music. The fans are frustrated by bullshit, they're looking for answers with clean edges. You know, get that anger release. Wear the band t-shirts out at the show before having to go back to their real lives, where it's all more complicated. Not as cool. Less empowering."

"So why do you do it?"

"Play music? Or... the stuff that led to this meeting?"

Another brief smile from Marcus. "You tell me. I'm listening."

"So, I'm not a college professor type," Glenn said. "Those guys write papers no one can understand—if they even get read. Me? Guys all over *the world* have heard my stuff. It resonates on a primal level. No need to explain jack shit with footnotes, either! Is that ego talking, or am I just one more fighter in that rumble of bodies trying to change the world?"

Marcus nodded. "To make it better. Keep it safe

from X, Y, and Z. Because we're all the good guy. And when there's no more villains—it's just an arms race of virtue."

"But now," Glenn said, blowing warm air into his hands, "after so many have fallen or bowed out, we see that maybe there isn't actually a championship belt. Or, it's not nearly as nice as we imagined it would be."

"And then what?" Marcus kicked at the dirt.

"Then you're home. Your dad's laid up on the couch in chronic pain. It's raining outside and some part of the roof is leaking. You realize that after all you've done to 'help'—while standing in the spotlight you pointed at yourself—you still haven't been able to escape that silent void. Which is what? Death… decay… or God?"

Marcus kneaded a fist inside the palm of his other hand. Slowly, he said, "Glenn, how much do you know about the Church of Modestianity?"

"Some. But I do know that the man in charge, uh… that he and I have a common interest."

"That may be so," Marcus said, matching Glenn's gaze, "but that's not why I ask. I shouldn't tell you this, Glenn, but last summer I was covertly embedded at the Mall of Absolution to keep an eye on things. Nothing nefarious, mind you. Just a precaution."

"Sure," Glenn said, "you were *helping* to protect people from themselves."

"I was just following orders," Marcus said with a shrug. "But along the way, something about it clicked with me. Whether *I* was missing something, or if it was the Prescient One's warnings about surveillance… Glenn, I found myself actually converting to Modestianity, and violating the trust of my bosses in the process."

"So, what… you've been tracking me as a free agent?"

"No, sir! They dragged my ass back in. Made me a deal. Said if I helped them land a big fish, they'd consider overlooking my… conflicting loyalties."

Glenn nodded. "And I'm that fish?"

"You got it."

"Speaking of loyalties then," Glenn said, "tell me this before you arrest me. How does race affect how you follow orders?"

Marcus titled his head. "What exactly are you getting at?"

"You're black, man! And what I've been doing lately… Heh, well, it certainly isn't helping your side."

"Ah, yes." Marcus let out a little chuckle. "We can't outrun—or outperform—our identities. The paint job. Especially not now when the government is involved. We're constantly reminded of… not who we *are*, but who came before us."

"Yeah." Glenn scratched his beard. "But you know something? I think MARVIN is a bit narrow-minded. When's he gonna toss us Irish guys a few crumbs?"

"You might be on to something there! If the Brits have to pay India back, why not their own neighbors?"

They both laughed.

"Oh man, once that gets going," Glenn said, "maybe they'll call it the Reparations East India Company. Start a whole new form of international trade. Then it'll never end."

Marcus wagged a finger. "Not until the last SOB who cut me off in traffic has to pay for his crime."

"Alright, I got it. You're not in love with what's going on."

"Glenn, I'm a cop. A lawyer. And before that I was a ball player. You made the squad by turning double plays, not by asking the runners to go back to the dugout on their own."

"But what about the guys who got cut from the team?" Glenn asked sarcastically. "They've got feelings. And families, too."

"Who the hell wants to watch a shitty baseball game?" Marcus sighed. "Look, I'm a quarter-white anyway. So I guess my loyalties have been divided since the day my parents or grandparents fell in love. I don't have the patience—or computing power—to figure it all out. Try as we might to let how we live as individuals determine our worth, someone's always got that hook ready to yank us back into the pen. But I can't fight *every* battle. So I do my job, try to be true to myself, and then hope for the best."

Glenn rubbed his hands together. "So is it time to do your job now? With me?"

"Christ, I don't know," Marcus muttered. "I really just do not know."

The two men stared at each other for a moment.

"So what's gonna happen?" Glenn said. "Can't stand here until the sun disappears."

"Shit..." Marcus said. "It's been good talking to you, Glenn. Couple of guys just hashing it all out... But now it's back to the world."

"It used to be," Glenn said, "that maybe a person could really hide away. But now drones and satellites and microphones and cameras are keeping tabs on every damn thing. We *have to* play a part at all times, because no one's safe even in their own bedroom! When does that act become more of who you are than the truth you've been hiding?"

Marcus suddenly brought his hands to the top of his head. "I have to take you in," he said. "But... I have to let you go."

Glenn folded his arms, then let them fall away. He said, "I made my choice months ago. Now you have to make yours."

"But I did choose!" Marcus said. "When I became a Modestian I also betrayed the FBI. Betrayed my oath. But they were willing to forgive if I would *help* them track down your network."

"Hmm. How concrete is the evidence you have against me?"

Marcus twisted his mouth. "Circumstantial. But the heightened state of alert means we could take you into custody, at least temporarily."

"So if you turn a blind eye," Glenn said, "someone else'll be right on my ass?"

"The president almost lost the election over all this. So yeah, I don't think the heat's gonna die down anytime soon."

"The hell with it," Glenn grumbled. "I've got to take the fall."

"Are you serious?" Marcus said.

"And not just for those people out there, either. I'll do it for you, too."

"*Me?*"

"Who can have more of an effect, me or you? There's already other people bringing supplies out to the caves. But you, a reformed Modestian back on the job? You could play any number of roles going forward."

"Damn, damn…" Marcus was amazed at Glenn's courage. "Alright. I'll bring you in. But away from here. I don't want those people who are hiding to be found."

"Exactly," Glenn said. "Follow me back a ways. I'll pull over somewhere."

"Even better," Marcus said, opening the car door and pulling out his official map. "There's a small NSA relay station about twenty miles from here. That's where I'll slap on the cuffs."

"Perfect. I just gotta dump this garbage out of the truck somewhere along the way."

Marcus nodded. As they moved to get back into the vehicles, he said, "And Glenn. I'll never forget what you did today."

Glenn Murray gave a wry smile.

"I've been provoking the system for a long time. Now we'll finally see who's gonna win."

30. THE LONELIEST REVELATION

"I just knew it was you. The whole time, I could feel it."

"Then why did you wait so long?"

"Believe me, I wanted to act. But other voices prevailed. Urging patience, caution, timing. The presumption of innocence!"

"So why now then?"

President Eileen Jeffries-Lao looked into the man's eyes and said, "Because *I won*. Now we have four years to set my legacy in stone—and no one can be allowed to get in the way. All of your Sentinel cronies have been rounded up, of course, but perhaps you thought you'd escaped detection?"

The man, his left wrist shackled to a chrome table in this sparse interrogation room, shrugged his shoulders.

"Mod only knows," he said, "what tomorrow holds."

Jeffries-Lao laughed, then wagged her finger. "Come now, Scott. Surely a *prescient* man such as yourself would have seen this coming, no?"

"And what if I had? Then *you* would be the one who fell into *my* trap."

"Are you serious?" Eileen stepped closer. "You, locked in a secure facility unknown to the outside world, while I have the means at my disposal to raze your precious Mall straight to the ground."

The Prescient One frowned. His face had been stripped of all putty and makeup shortly after his initial capture a week ago. Even his signature blue outfit had been replaced by the hideous orange jumpsuit of a common criminal. He was, for all intents and purposes, Scott Cullen once again.

President Jeffries-Lao, for her part, wore a power outfit of sky-blue blouse tucked into a gray pencil skirt that was belted tightly about the waist. Her three-inch heels were stacked, as much for balance as to stomp loudly when needed.

"You wouldn't do that," Cullen said. "It would create a humanitarian—and public relations—disaster."

Eileen kept her eyes on him as she walked a slow circle. "Not if we ran with the story that your whole church was a breeding ground for subversives. Home base of the hacker cult!"

The man jangled his cuffed wrist. He said, "You could do that. And get away with it as well. But perhaps my foresight had also accounted for that."

"Are you playing games with me?" Jeffries-Lao's voice echoed through the room.

"I wouldn't dare."

The president exhaled slowly. "So tell me then, what *is* your endgame? And don't get cute. Because, you know, I could have my guards kill you under the pretense that you'd endangered my life." Eileen motioned toward the two Secret Servicemen who were standing in opposite corners of the room. "I'm telling you right now, it's time to lay all your cards out on the table."

"Eileen," Scott said, "if I may call you that… How old were you when you got your first cell phone?"

She smiled. "Okay, I'll play along. It was around the time I finished college, so about thirty years ago. Why?"

"How often did you use it?"

"Well," Eileen said, "all you could do in those days was make phone calls, so not very often."

"Indeed. You're about ten years older than me, and by the time I turned twenty-one, smartphones were on the march. Texting had graduated to web browsing, video chat, email, music… A whole life right in the palm of your hand."

"Yes, yes," the president said impatiently. "And it only kept evolving into the indispensable tool we have today. But what is your point?"

The Prescient One made as if to rise, looked at his shackles, then leaned back into the chair. Deliberately he began, "Everyone is familiar with the story of my fall from grace three years ago. As well as the profound vision in exile that guided me to where I… was at least until recently. But years and years before that, during the height of my success with *Thor's Tablet*, I remember seeing a young woman—she was stunning, with pale skin and long brown hair… But she was so engrossed in her phone that she looked like a hunchback! It was a nightmare! Voluntary scoliosis. In that moment I was absolutely horrified, because I too was contributing to the digital addiction that continues to lure people away from nature in a million ways. Of course, I was also a young man back then, and life excitement soon distracted me from that moment of clarity. But I've never forgotten it."

"A touching memory, I'm sure," Jeffries-Lao said. "But what does that have to do with the predicament you're in today?"

"Because, madam," the prisoner said, "despite my church's best efforts to reacquaint people with real life —by planting gardens and singing freely—I fear that humanity's next reaction will not be to abandon the void of the artificial world at all. No, in order to fully escape the scrutiny state which *you* oversee—this living hell where surveillance conspires with punitive measures— people will dive in *deeper* via full immersion. Perhaps with some combination of float tanks, neural implants, and feeding tubes... Any method to renounce the body and protect the mind—and all this by choice! Then they will again be free to love, grow, make mistakes, be *human* in a way that is now denied to them under the all-seeing eye. Perhaps we will call that new state of existence, Screen Rapture!

"And Eileen," the man continued, "if your legacy is truly what fuels you, please remember my warning: MARVIN and the Reparations program could *accelerate* this ultimate form of self-segregation. Where each man, woman, and child chooses to hide away alone, for fear of what humiliation and punishments might befall their imperfect fleshly lives."

Jeffries-Lao shook her head doubtfully. She chuckled. "Ah yes, the silver tongue of the cult leader. But it's always been about the negative side of things with you. Crying wolf for years now, in fact. Just consider this though, Scott. Sometimes what we call accountability isn't all that far removed from your punishment bogeyman. I'd rather we shine *more* disinfecting sunlight onto the world, than the alternative of continuing to sweep inconvenient facts under the rug."

Scott Cullen smiled softly. "And *I* just knew you would say something to that effect. What I've tried to do with Modestianity is put up a roadblock, or pave a new path as best I could. But," he said, eyes twinkling for the first time in days, "you might get exactly what you want in the end."

*　　*　　*

Eileen Jeffries-Lao had signaled for refreshments to be brought in. After a rolling cart with food and beverages arrived, she sat on the edge of the table holding a small sandwich plate.

"Scott," she said, "do you really think you're more qualified to lay out a vision for the future than me?"

"It's not a matter of qualifications," the man shackled to the table said.

"No? I'm president today because I took the proper steps while working within the system for many years. I proved that I was a steady hand, a team player when needed, and all the while was still able to keep my core vision intact. But you," Eileen said, wiping her mouth before tossing a crumpled napkin onto the table, "you ping pong from lark to lark, just doing whatever strikes your fancy. And always relying on your so-called genius, when maybe you're nothing more than an Elmer Gantry. Using the salesman's cleverness to convince people to pony up money, or indeed, devote their lives to a new church. So yes, I do think the nation would be wiser to lean on me and my team of vetted professionals."

The Prescient One took the discarded napkin with his free hand and brushed several crumbs off the table surface, then put it into his jumpsuit pocket.

"Again," he said, "I believe there is more than one

path to... Well, what is all this about? Knowledge? Experience? A person becoming the total package? Because maybe relying on job titles and certifications is a religious faith of its own. Yes, the cult of credentialism! And what distinguishes your kind from mine, is that people like me scare you to death."

"Absurd!" Eileen cracked open a soda can and stomped away from the table. "You are truly a reckless and dangerous individual. So in that way, I very much *would* fear your type fiddling with the levers of power. We've already seen how nervous an unstable president can make the rest of the world."

"No, no," Cullen said sharply. "What you find appalling is the realization that someone might make it to the same level of authority or wisdom as you, but without the humiliation you endured as down payment. Kneeling to kiss the ring. Turning a blind eye here, turning the other cheek there. Oh yes, I navigated the same world as you, but without having to sell my soul."

"I'd rather lose a few chunks on this righteous mission," the president snarled, "than completely fall apart as you have. Sir, you wear glitter and prosthetic glue on your face as a selling point!"

Scott Cullen rubbed a hand against his bare skin, then raised his eyebrows.

"You know, Madam President, the most dangerous thing that a self-made millionaire can do is turn away from hedonism and start pulling back the curtain of the world. Because in truth, I figured out a few things early on, but still had enough to believe in that I could disregard those uncomfortable ideas. But when you and yours cast me aside, destroyed my reputation... Well, you can guess the rest. Out of that madness and disillusionment, I first found a new purpose for myself —and then came a comprehensive understanding of how it all really works."

"Oh?" Eileen scoffed. "Do tell! I might need to take some notes."

"Maybe you should," the Prescient One said. "It's actually why in the end I can't hate you. Because I know you're just one of the more gilded pawns on this global stage. While I may not see the entire picture, I surely know more than you—because you've been rewarded for conforming all this time. Mrs. Jeffries-Lao, you only masquerade as a leader."

The president thought for a moment. She said, "I may have conformed, as you say. But what's wrong with that if, in the end, you're on the right side? That blinding shine you see on me is *confidence*. No nervous ticks like the eccentric you are."

"Optics aside," Cullen said, "so-called eccentrics like me do the work of going down all the different rabbit holes. Then we piece that random data together on our own. Which of course turns out to be so ludicrously ironic."

Eileen was back at the food cart taking nibbles of chopped fruit. She looked up and said, "I promise you, I'm writing in my mind. Keep going, please."

"Certainly. Take that old sales pitch from Apple computers. 'Think different.' It's a nice sentiment for children, but what happens in real life? You come back proudly holding up what you found, but then people cover their eyes and scream, 'No, no! We didn't *really* mean for you to think different!' The truth is, if you just want to be weird on the surface, that's fine. They'll pay you handsomely as long as you go with the flow. But don't call the plan into question, otherwise they have to rewrite everything."

Eileen Jeffries-Lao, who had been shaking her head with a smirk, now said, "You see me as some kind of globalist shill, don't you? Well, Mr. Cullen, I'll have you know that what I've done with the HRA, is to pour the concrete foundation for something that will live on writ large for decades to come. And history will remember who was on the captain's bridge when humanity finally began to move forward *together*. Meanwhile you… This Modestianity nonsense will turn out to be nothing more than a did-you-know footnote in children's textbooks."

"What's the point in comparing my legacy to yours?" the Prescient One asked. "I fell into prominence—*you* sought it out! Had my concerns about MARVIN been addressed, then I would have remained a quiet techie behind the scenes, perhaps consulting remotely from time to time while off building my next business idea. As for this talk of uniting humanity, you're not speaking to a supporter-dupe out on the campaign trail. I know very well that your worldwide Reparations expansion is already floundering."

"My god!" Jeffries-Lao let out a near-scream. "You fool! We've got alliances with over a dozen countries already in place. And I assure you, plenty more are waiting in line right behind them."

"This is a farce!" Scott shook his head and laughed. "That roster of small colonies is birdseed compared to China or Russia. The grand imperial powers want *nothing* to do with outsiders looking into their archives."

"My, what a short memory you have," Eileen said. "It was we who won the Cold War. And my embarrassing predecessor does deserve credit for the strong trade policies that reigned China in. Before you say anything, no, I am not beholden to the land of my ancestors. Because as you are well aware, my husband is Caucasian."

"Good old Paul, yes. The Jeffries in Jeffries-Lao!"

Eileen nodded patiently.

"Thank you for remembering," she said. "Now, Scott. These countries may be physically bigger than England, which is fully on board with paying Reparations, but I assure you they are still *weak*. Dysfunction at every level. If they and their billions of people have any hope of being relevant this century… If they want a chance at order, unity, peace, being there as mankind explores the stars…"

For the first time, the Prescient One looked surprised. "What *are* you getting at?" he nearly shouted.

"I am telling you," Eileen said, "why they will eventually acquiesce and join us. Because it's all so much bigger than countries—and yes, even race. Therefore what is money in this context? Bait? A tool, or a device used to persuade? And in that regard, maybe I *am* just a well-fed pawn on the world stage, as you say. So be it. Because as you now see, this project goes far beyond the scope of Reparations. That's just one stepping stone helping to vault us all toward the kind of cooperation needed to fulfill humanity's dream of seeding other planets. What do you say to that, sir? Do you not now finally begin to feel some shame because your own terroristic actions worked against such a noble venture?"

The Prescient One was momentarily stunned. He shuddered, then finally said, "The ends always justify the means, don't they? The lies, the cover-ups. And the steamrolling of uncomfortable ethical concerns. But now I see just how far people like you are willing to go to keep the candle of that messianic faith burning."

Eileen stared daggers at him. "*You* would dare call me out as a messiah? Ha! I never looked the part. I never played the part. That's your area of expertise. You have followers. I have allies. You speak *to* your people—I speak *for* mine."

"I might actually believe that," Scott said, "if you hadn't just blurted out that whole space travel manifesto. No one who voted for you and the Reparations ticket ever imagined that the HRA could be used to bring about some sort of worldwide NASA alliance."

Eileen inspected one of her cuticles. Dropping her hand away she said, "It's true that they might not have the wide-angle lens for such an all-encompassing grand vision. But I bet you, ninety-nine percent of them hope to colonize the stars just as much as they support equity."

"Ah, colonizing." The Prescient One closed his eyes and nodded. He said, "First you will ensure that Earth is completely homogenized. Then we will go out and plant our flag somewhere else. Until what—one day all of humanity owes Reparations to the planets and moons we disturbed and imposed our will upon? Wiped out with our strange diseases?"

"Beyond ludicrous! Truly, Scott, you've outdone yourself. I'm speechless."

"Because you realize you just stepped in it. You're so mentally ill that you could watch a million or fifty million people die in conflicts about the past, as long as Mars got terraformed in the process. But I say no!" Scott Cullen was fuming. "Your lens is completely flipped. We aren't supposed to keep spreading out. We need to get simpler, more intimate, quieter, and slow down. Because we as a species are *exhausted!* We've all been smashed together, lurched from horses to jet planes... but still the creeping dread of some nameless malaise hounds us.

"And I know," Cullen continued, "that we won't be able to escape it in deep space, either. We might succeed in ignoring this doubt for a while—keep everyone so busy *doing* what it takes to build the ships to get us out there. But eventually the bustle ends, and then we're left with ourselves again. It'll be the loneliest revelation ever—half a million miles from home."

President Eileen Jeffries-Lao began to clap sarcastically. "A touching warning, thank you. But I'm sorry, we simply can't afford to wait. Not with all the tools at our fingertips—and a few great leaders who are prepared for this moment. Those who have the stomach and the courage to do what is necessary. These opportunities are so rare that we are *obligated* to seize them. In that light, what you have done might be unforgivable. I wish I was ruthless enough to have you killed right now."

Cullen looked up. Eileen was staring at him, hands on hips, beautifully vicious. He said, "But you still need me for something, perhaps?"

She exhaled slowly. "Yes, I suppose I do. A great mind is a terrible thing to waste, after all."

"If only I would go along with the plan, right?"

"It's called staying in your lane!" Jeffries-Lao shouted, but then calmed herself. She said, "You're a technician, not a politician."

"That may be so," Scott said, "but I think your fervor has bled over into fanaticism. You never revealed those sharp teeth out on the campaign trail."

"Me, a fanatic? Mr. Cullen, I do believe you are the pot calling the kettle... teal."

Eileen smiled with self-satisfaction.

Scott Cullen straightened his posture and said, "The difference, Madam President, is that I have always been forthright. And beyond the teal and gray,

Modestianity's intentions are wholly transparent. You, however, secretly hide the ambition of a would-be immortal behind a deal maker's calm smile."

"If not me," Jeffries-Lao declared, "someone else would have filled the role!"

"I know!" Cullen whacked the table with his cuffed hand. "And that's a great danger for us all. There are tens of millions of aspiring messiahs who hide behind the title of 'activist' or 'advocate.' All salivating for the moment when *they* hold the power to manipulate entire nations. I use my words to enrich, rather than twist the minds of others."

"But Scott, everything that you see in the world came about through molding and manipulation. Land, objects, people—all changed by invention, war, and yes, even that word you must dread, *policy*. It can't be stopped. All we can decide is who steers the ship."

The Prescient One looked down at his bright jumpsuit for a moment. He said finally, "You've devoted all this time and effort to one man—me. Why, Eileen? Why exactly are you here today? You've got an entire nation to spy on, a Reparations program to run, and apparently a spaceship to steer!"

"Because," Jeffries-Lao answered coldly, "twice you have tried to derail me and the progressive vanguard that I serve. From the Beneficiaries to their allies, you have threatened and nearly broken the hearts of countless people across this country. To think that one rudderless man could become so filled with spite, just because someone took away his door key. That he would allow the gift of his brilliant mind to be so perverted, and then seek to chop down a nationwide movement at the knees! No, Mr. Cullen, I cannot let you continue to put any more Americans at risk. It is now time, in fact, for you to be punished."

"What do you intend to do?" Scott asked quietly.

Eileen Jeffries-Lao leaned forward onto the table, then pointed a finger directly at his face.

"I want to know," she said, "what really drives a man to invent a new god, and them appoint himself as the conduit. Is it ego? Or is there a gaping hole in his heart that he could never fill? A successful man like you... But you don't really know what it is, do you? Your *Prescience*, you still haven't figured out how it all came to this. But that's okay. We'll get to the bottom of it. No resources or pain receptors will be spared, you treasonous bastard!"

The President of the United States turned on her heel and motioned to the two Secret Servicemen standing guard.

A moment later Scott Cullen, aka the Prescient One, was alone to contemplate his fate.

31. UNCHAINED

The *DDM TV Live* studio audience clapped along in time with a rousing big band number as Ryan Richards strutted onto the stage. His shimmering navy blue suit was accented by a gray shirt and snowman-print necktie.

"Wow," Richards said. "Can you believe it's December already? After everything that we've been through together this year—the ups and the downs—let's take a moment to remember that we're still here. *Breathe!* We are alright. Now," he said, pumping a fist, "let's get this episode started with a bang!"

A snare drum roll slowly built to a crescendo as a TV screen was lowered to stage level beside him. Cymbals crashed and the face of a distinguished elderly man appeared on the screen.

Ryan Richards studied the picture thoughtfully for a moment, then said, "This is Cornelius Alemán. Do any of you know who that is? Have you even *heard* his name before?"

Murmurs of doubt came from the crowd. Richards

flashed a mischievous smile.

"No?" he asked, slowly letting the vowel fall away. "He's *only* among the top two hundred wealthiest people in the world! Oil and gas interests, global shipping… oh, and he's been known to dabble in, how shall I say it? Media… politics… the fate of nations!

"Ladies and gentlemen," Richards continued, his voice now working into a frenzied lather, "he is the Mexican George Soros! Anywhere around the world you look, you'll see Alemán bucks in action. An Argentinian newspaper rescued from insolvency. Movies financed in the Philippines, but only when the language spoken is Spanish! And of course, a generous endowment for Latiz-American scholarships right here at home. But… But, but, but!!!"

The host wagged a finger at the photograph.

"Even this polished scion of the noble Alemán dynasty has secrets. Secrets, secrets…" Richards whispered. "Only talked about in hushed tones by those fearful of his wrath. Oh, if you only knew. Guards!" Ryan shouted. "Bring him… to me!"

The host put hands on hips and stuck out his chest as three giant men in black cargo fatigues prodded the elderly man forward. Silver shackles that were linked by a vertical chain bound the newcomer's hands and ankles.

Nervous sounds from the audience mixed with the low rumble of orchestral bass drums thumping through the studio speakers. No guest had ever appeared on the show restrained in this manner. People were asking themselves, just how dangerous *was* this man?

Alemán maintained his dignified composure. Despite the humiliating double chains, he had at least been permitted to wear slacks and a blazer instead of a prisoner's jumpsuit.

As the guards spread out to different corners of the stage, Ryan Richards took the opportunity to playfully inspect the man. Finally he drew back and said, "Cornelius Alemán, ask not for whom the spreadsheet tolls—today it tolls for thee!"

A gong sounded from somewhere. Alemán held his ground as Richards tried to nudge him closer to the TV screen.

"Look at these stats," Richards said, shaking his head sadly at the charts which detailed the man's genetic breakdown. "*Eighty-eight percent* Western European DNA. And yet you masquerade as a champion of the Latizo people? Shame on you, sir."

In the silence that followed, Alemán raised his eyebrows at Richards, who nodded back.

The old man said, "My name is Cornelius Gomez de Vallarta Alemán. I am a respected US citizen. I have been abducted from my home in Vermont and dragged here on trumped-up political charges. Shame on all of you for being a part of this disgraceful charade."

Alemán winced at the barrage of boos and catcalls that followed this declaration of innocence. Ryan Richards flashed his trademark smirk and said, "I don't think they like you, Corn Dog. And they haven't even been presented with the evidence yet."

"What evidence, you… court jester?!"

Richards brought a hand to his chest, then grimaced as he said, "Who, little old me?"

"We love you, Ryan!" a female voice called out from the darkened seating area.

"Thank you, my dear," he replied, loosening up for a moment before putting on a stern expression and again facing his guest. "To Mr. Alemán and everyone here tonight, I ask that you all turn your attention to the video screens—hard as it might be to stomach."

A series of disturbing images began to cycle through. There were black-and-white photographs of dead bodies, charred ruins, and groups of men holding rifles.

"And there it is," Richards said gravely. "Over three thousand killings during the Mexican Revolution attributed directly to the Alemán clan. Men, women, children—even the livestock when their farms were burned to the ground. Horrible, just horrible!" Richards moaned. "There are no words."

Alemán's poise finally broke down. "This is outrageous!" he thundered. "You cannot in hindsight impose the niceties of peacetime upon a nation that was in the throes of a civil war. To cherry pick one anecdote from a decade-long struggle, where both sides suffered terrible losses…"

"Just as a law court holds one trial at a time," Richards said, "so too can *DDM TV* only film one episode at a time. And as anyone can see, our docket is full! Backlogged with the likes of you, who would deny or explain away their Bloodline Crimes!"

The audience was torn between somber grief for the victims and a boiling desire for vengeance against Cornelius Alemán.

"What the hell do you want then?" the old man said contemptuously. "I am familiar with the nature of this preposterous television program. Who will you bring out here in hopes that I would grovel at their feet for forgiveness?"

Ryan Richards dropped his head, shaking it slowly. "No," he said, "there's no one."

"Good!"

"It is not good, *sir*. The reason being that entire lineages were wiped out in these massacres. And the few ultra-distant relatives MARVIN did find in the system were simply too afraid to make the long journey —even with all expenses paid by our proud sponsor, Total Comfort Airlines."

"So," Cornelius said, "these people don't even live in the United States? What in the name of God am I doing on this stage bound in chains? Oh... I see now. This isn't about justice, or healing anything. You are trying to discredit *me*. Destroy my reputation, derail my charitable efforts. Did... did she put you up to this?"

Richards drew back dramatically with widened eyes. "*She?*" he said.

"Your president, of course," the old man grunted.

"Well," Ryan stammered, "I'm just the host here, not the producer..."

"Witch-hunt!" Alemán screamed and raised his shackled fists above his head. "You are all witnessing a political lynching."

Ryan Richards stiffened. "Now, now, mister! Let's not go throwing around culturally sensitive terms. You know what? I've had enough. Guards, just get him off my stage..."

"This is a travesty!" Cornelius cried. "You people in the audience, look what they're doing here. Not even obeying the rules of their own show. Will you just sit there and take it? I am being judged without the ability to even face my accuser!"

Now the studio audience was on its feet, angry at both Alemán for his Bloodline Crimes and the show for not following its normal course of conflict resolution. Ryan Richards stepped forward and motioned for them to calm down.

"Fear not, *DDM* fans," he said with a confident smile. "Because come on, this is *me* you're dealing with here. Ryan Patrick Richards, the captain of this proud ship! Mr. Alemán, do you *really* want a showdown?"

The elderly man gave a chilling smile that rivaled any of Ryan's own top-ten grins. "It's the only way," he said.

"So be it," the host replied. "Ladies and gentlemen, behold... the plaintiff!"

A middle-aged Latizo man wearing a beige suit came into view. He saluted with great fervor as he walked across the stage. Recognition slowly dawned on the crowd—this face had been a staple of the news cycle for more than a year.

But applause was not forthcoming. Here was the man who had insinuated his desire to rein in the HRA if elected president. What damage might he have also done to this popular television show?

"You traitor!" Cornelius Alemán howled as the man came near.

Ryan Richards struck a dramatic pose as he swung from left to right, and said, "Welcome to the show, Senator Victor Dominguez! Sorry-not-sorry about your loss last month. But no hard feelings! Now, what do you have to say to our friend Cornelius?"

The senator brushed Ryan away with a wave and fixed a hard gaze upon the old man. "No, Mr. Alemán," he declared. "It is *you* who is the traitor. Or should I say... infiltrator?!"

At this accusation, the show host fell flat on his back as if bowled over by a raging bull. The crowd stood up again and gave a loud cheer—finally there was blood in the water.

Richards scrambled to his feet and sidled up against Cornelius. He said, "Mr. Alemán, that is quite the indictment. What say you, sir?"

"I am a public figure known and highly regarded around the world," the old man declared indignantly. "It is outrageous to slander me like this."

"The floor is yours, Victor," Ryan Richards said. "What have you got to back up your claims?"

Senator Dominguez pointed a stern finger and said, "I may not have won the presidency, but God has now given me an even greater opportunity. To prevent the country from being torn apart by this man right here!"

Richards leaped forward and threw a left-right punch combo into the air. "Ouch!" he gasped, then imitated a ring announcer as he said, "That one stunned him, Frank! Will Victor go for the knockout, or just toy with him for a while?"

Dominguez looked askance at the host, then continued, "Ladies and gentlemen, there are differences, and then there are *differences*. Dramacrats and Rebellicans may disagree over political ideas—and yes, the rhetoric has gotten quite vicious over the past decade. But I believe deeply that we still have enough in common to sit on the patio and enjoy a sunset together."

Ryan Richards batted his eyes and placed a hand on his breast.

"But this man," Victor continued, "wants to tap into the worst aspects of tribal thinking in order to consolidate his own power. Cornelius Alemán uses nice-sounding phrases like 'Latizo Pride,' but not to gain more appreciation for our people, as a new national holiday might do. He rejects *E pluribus unum* in favor of only one race rising to the top of the melting pot. My oath to the Constitution—and my heart— cannot abide by such anti-American sentiments."

Ryan Richards staggered back, his head wobbling as if stung by an uppercut. "Cornelius," he pleaded in a raspy voice, "you've got to fight back. Throw a punch, or it's over!"

Cornelius Alemán yanked at the lapels of his blazer,

shackles clattering loudly as he did so.

He said, "I am ashamed of you, Victor. To think that I ever had faith in you. That you would so fawn over being an American. You short-sighted fool! You turncoat! We are descendants of the greatest empire the world has seen in a thousand years—the Spanish Empire! Lasting far longer than the British, and today our language and architecture live on around the globe.

"What *is* this worship of the United States all about?" Cornelius implored. "Why do people hold such reverence for a leftover from the skirmishes between European powers? It is a wasteland where all genetic stock is perpetually wrecked against the rocks of disorganized breeding! So am I *really* a traitor? Or just the latest visionary to try his hand at remaking the landscape? What, are you shocked by my candor? Your own president is less than seventy-five years removed from the rice paddies of China! Yet you don't think it's possible that *her* foreign ties could influence any of her policies?"

Ryan Richards choked for words amid the din of the audience's screams and howls. Victor Dominguez took a step forward and motioned for silence.

He said, "Not long ago, Eileen Jeffries-Lao and I were fierce ideological combatants. But do you know what we have in common? We both married outside of our races. My wife Jaclyn is fifty-percent white, one-quarter Navajo, and one-quarter Hispanic. And First Man Paul Jeffries, who I respect very much, is a full-blooded WASP whose family goes all the way back to this country's colonial beginnings. All of our children are *one-hundred-percent* American! And that is why I chose to stand up in full opposition to the Alemán Conspiracy."

Richards smacked his forehead audibly. "A...

conspiración?! Senator, please forgive me. I misjudged you. A truer patriot I've never known."

"I'm just thankful for this chance to lay out the truth," Victor said with a bow.

Ryan Richards whipped his arm in the direction of Cornelius Alemán. "Guards, guards!" he called out. "Seize this creepy old geezer and take him away."

As the men in fatigues dragged a struggling Cornelius Alemán off the stage, he wailed, "You can silence me. You can jail me. But you cannot stop our rising tide! The future is Latizzzzz…"

The roars of the frothing crowd drowned out Ryan's attempts to speak. Everyone was simply too riled up after the most shocking outcome in the show's two-year history. Again it was Victor Dominguez who patiently lowered his arms until all was quiet.

"Thank you, ladies and gentlemen," he said. "After such high drama, perhaps we can all go home tonight as better people. Wiser and more compassionate. God bless you and the United States of America."

Dominguez quickly shook the host's hand before turning and walking toward the side of the stage.

"Uh… Not so fast, Senator."

Ryan Richards stood there with his arms folded, a wicked smile on his lips.

Victor stopped and turned his head back slowly. "Excuse me?"

"We've actually got some unfinished business here."

"Really? Like what?"

Richards motioned for Dominguez to come closer.

"Victor," he said, "you're from Arizona. So surely you know that large swaths of the American Southwest were once part of Mexico."

"Yes, of course." Victor was now standing beside the host.

"There was also an independent Republic of Texas for nearly ten years."

Dominguez smiled as he said, "Did you know that Sam Houston actually served as its president on two separate occasions?"

"Really now?" Ryan said. "Well, since you're so familiar with that country's history, tell me this. Does the name Salvador 'El Diablo' Colon ring a bell?"

Victor froze. He licked his lips. "Oh, no…"

"Oh, yes!" Richards exclaimed. "A little naughty, naughty during the Mexican-American War! Victor, we know you were vetted before the election, so I can only assume that new ancestral connections have been made *south of the border*. And with such nastiness in your genetic past, it looks like America really dodged a bullet this past November."

The sound of a large dog barking began to play over the PA system.

"Hey Victor, do you hear that?" Ryan said.

"What's going on?" Sweat was beading on Dominguez's forehead.

"It's MARVIN," Ryan whispered. "I think he broke free."

"Broke free?"

"Oh my God!" Richards howled. "Ladies and gentlemen, MARVIN's on the loose! MARVIN, stop that! Come here, right now. That's a good boy, yes… No! Bad MARVIN, *bad!* Uh-oh… I don't know if I can hold him much longer…"

Ryan Richards fell to his knees as the barking receded into the distance.

"Run for your lives, everyone! I think he's got rabies. He could be coming for you next! MARVIN has been… unchained!!!"

THE END.

BUT THE STORY CONTINUES

IN THE FOURTH AND FINAL CHAPTER…

REPARATIONS MAZE!

ABOUT THE AUTHOR

Originally from Northern Virginia, Philip Wyeth has lived in the Los Angeles area for many years. He's an entrepreneur, musician, film aficionado, hockey fan, and enjoys playing tennis and golf.

Inspired by such unique writers as Heinrich von Kleist, Ambrose Bierce, Joseph Conrad, and Len Deighton, Wyeth's imaginative novels will resonate with fans of Philip K. Dick, Rich Larson, Michel Houellebecq, and Neal Stephenson.

Also a lifelong fan of heavy metal music and its many sub-genres, Wyeth strives to infuse his writing with comparable levels of intensity, independence, and larger-than-life visions.

His website is www.philipwyeth.com, and you can follow him across the social media landscape under the following handles:

@PhilipWyeth: Twitter, BitChute, Gab, and Minds.

@PhilipWyethWriter: Instagram and Facebook.